Harboring Secrets

Tales & Reflections
from
The Chesapeake Bay Writers

An anthology of work celebrating the
20th Anniversary of
The Chesapeake Bay Writers

ISBN 978-1-937556-05-1

First Edition 2013

Cover design by Braxton McGhee

Published by:
Cherokee McGhee, L.L.C.
Williamsburg, Virginia

Find us on the World Wide Web at:
www.CherokeeMcGhee.com

Printed in the United States of America

Harboring Secrets

Tales & Reflections
from
The Chesapeake Bay Writers

To Charlene,
Enjoy! Julie Severine

Hope you enjoy the stories!
Greg Lilly

Edited by
Narielle Living & Greg Lilly

Cherokee McGhee

Williamsburg, Virginia

To Charlou,
Enjoy!

Contents

FROM THE EDITORS

NARIELLE LIVING & GREG LILLY

Harboring Secrets
Tales & Reflections from the Chesapeake Bay Writers

An anthology of work celebrating the
20th Anniversary of the Chesapeake Bay Writers

Anthologies are a vehicle to showcase established writers along with new, up-and-coming writers. This anthology spotlights the talent in the Chesapeake Bay Writers club. The editors selected the best submissions, and although only a small number were chosen, each writer gained experience in the publishing process.

We looked for the craft of writing paired with the art of storytelling. The Chesapeake Bay Writers club, like writers' groups all over the world, meets to hone our skills and further our proficiency in writing. We learn our trade from each other as well as from hours of practice.

There is no guildhall; we write in cafés, libraries, coffeehouses, living rooms, boat docks, and porches. We listen to the conversations of our friends, families, and strangers to incorporate moments of truth into our tales, maybe discovering a few secrets to share.

Our theme for this anthology is: Harboring Secrets. Our setting is the Chesapeake Bay region of Virginia. *New York*

Times bestselling author John Gilstrap writes about the Power of Secrets in our introduction. This theme allowed the writers to soar with their creativity. While exploring the idea of "secrets," the authors may have given away a few of their own – that's for the readers to determine.

The contributors' works represent a broad range of genres. You'll find short fiction, personal essays, poetry, mystery, children's fiction, fantasy, paranormal, romance, memoir, and science fiction.

We hope you enjoy the stories. Think of them the next time you see a county crew cutting down an old oak, watch a restored Skipjack glide across the York River, drive along the Colonial Parkway at night, hear a thump in your attic, or stumble across an abandoned airport in the woods. These are our secrets. We're listening to discover yours.

INTRODUCTION: THE POWER OF SECRETS

JOHN GILSTRAP

W ho among us has not longed to know the secrets kept by others? How does your neighbor afford the car he drives when he purports to live on a public servant's salary? Why is that man always smiling? Why does that woman never smile? What is your coworker really doing for three hours every day with his door closed?

And who among us would not go to great lengths to prevent the revelation of at least one secret in our own lives? Our secrets define us, allow us to shape for others the image that we want them to see, projecting our strengths and sheltering our weaknesses. Some secrets are so powerful that once revealed, fine reputations can be forever and indelibly tarnished. For some, those are the secrets worth killing others to protect.

Secrets may be small and tawdry, as in the case of a cheating spouse, or it can be massive in scope, as in the Watergate affair that toppled the Nixon presidency.

Still other secrets are heartbreaking. In November of 1940, when informed that the German Luftwaffe would bomb the city of Coventry, British Prime Minister Winston Churchill ordered that no warning be given in order to protect the source of valuable intelligence. Dozens of people died in that raid, and much of the city was left ablaze.

Was the cost of perpetuating such secrets worth the ultimate costs? Well, therein lies the human drama. Those who lost loved ones in the bombing probably take little solace in the fact that because of superior intelligence capabilities the Allies were able to win the war just months before my father would have been deployed to it. One could imagine that I am here today as a direct result of the Coventry sacrifice.

As I write this, secrets and their aftermath are very much in the news as we are all atwitter about revelations made by a man who according to many, should never have had access to the information in the first place. By any estimation, the effect of this recent disclosure will be to change the way intelligence is gathered in the future. Again, is this good or is this bad?

In the long run, the history books will judge.

But as a novelist, I don't have to wait for the history books. I make stuff up for a living, and in that context, I can make any spy a hero or a traitor—or both, through the prism of shifting points of view. In a novel, a secret is only as powerful as the force it exerts on the character who protects it.

In my novel *High Treason*, and in others of the thriller series I write, Jonathan Grave continually battles against those who would use secrets to the worst possible end. The stakes are huge. But at their heart, each of the stories is about individual characters struggling to survive and to prevail over difficult odds. In the end, the books are about these characters discovering the truth of who they truly are.

I believe that conflict is the single essential element of compelling fiction. Conflict can exist between characters, or between a character and his environment. The most meaningful conflict, though, is that which exists between a character and himself—the himself he projects to be or desires to be, vs. the himself he truly is.

Compelling drama lies in the fissures created between characters' dreams and their realities, between their truths and their fictions. As writers, our job is to mine those frailties and to create three dimensional human beings out of the ether of our imaginations. As craftsmen, we bear the responsibility for prolonging the achievement of each character's needs until the last possible moment. Longings that are suppressed or denied are dramatic, while longings that are expressed or accepted are boring.

This volume is all about secrets and the people who keep them—secrets worth dying and killing for. As you read through the stories and absorb the mysteries and the tortures of their protectors, take a moment to reflect on the skeletons in your own closet. Are they protected?

Are you sure?

John Gilstrap, *New York Times* bestselling author of
High Treason and *Nathan's Run*
Fairfax, Virginia
June, 2013

THE OAK TREE ON THE OLD POST ROAD

FRANK MILLIGAN

S oon's I walked into that doctor's office, I knew things was finally going to start going my way. That Dr. Samuels, he a fine handsome young man, remind you of Carey Hatcher's first born, young Winston. He so cute, trying to look all official and everything.

He says, "Mrs. Quarrels, do you understand the purpose of our session here today, why you're here?"

So I answer him straight out and truthful just like the public defender say I should. I say, "Yes sir. I here cause the judge remaindered me here."

I know I be okay now. Was the way he smile at me clinched it. He have that kind of smile go all the way up into his eyes, just like young Winston. He asks me how old I am, tells me it says in his papers, "around seventy nine." I tell him that's right. He says, "Well then, when will you be eighty?" I tell him probably never. Been around seventy nine for a couple of years, probably going to be around seventy nine for a couple more.

He says, trying hard to look doctorly, "We'll be taping our session, if you don't mind. For the record, you're here because the Chief Judge, Williamsburg and James City County District Court, remanded you for psychiatric evaluation to determine if you're competent to stand trial for the murder of Mr. Rawley Semans, bulldozer operator."

Remembering what the lawyer told me, I says, "Yes

sir, that's right. I kilt him all right, but like I been telling everybody, it was self-defense. He was going to kill my tree."

So he ask me to tell him bout my tree and I start telling him but then it hits me, maybe now things not going so well as they was, cause I start blatherin on bout my tree, and I see this look come in his eyes like he thinks maybe I am nuts, but I got to tell it to him, so I keep going.

I tell him about how that old oak was probably already a hundred years old the day I was born there in my daddy's house out on the Old Post Road. And I tell him bout how when I was a little girl I'd stand there next to that tree after a rainfall and drink in the smell of that heavy, sweet black soil, and dig my toes in, and share a drink of God's goodness with that tree, knowing it would make me grow up big and strong just like it. And then I told him bout how I first met Henry there, the year of the big drought.

I was sitting in the swing Daddy'd hung from a wide low branch and I see this swirl of dust coming up the Old Post Road, long before I can see what's causing it, and don't it turn out to be Henry, tall and strong and handsome, just moved in with his aunt, and for all of his twelve years old, in all that heat, peddling his bike like the hounds of hell nipping at his heels.

Well don't he take a notice of me sitting in that swing, and bring that bike to a skid and cause a cloud of dust make him look just like that fella in the magic show, appears out of a puff of smoke. He asks can he push me, and I say yes, and before long there's Henry's initials next to mine inside a big heart carved into that old tree and you can still see'em today if you know where to look.

And I told that doctor how I'll never forget the night Henry asked me to be his wife under that same tree. It's a warm spring evening and there's a full moon peeking its light through the leaves causing Henry's eyes to sparkle like they was full of thousands of little diamonds just like the one he's slipped on my finger. And when I tell him yes, all of a sudden a gust of wind comes and sweeps through those branches and it sounds like the tree is sighing just for us and we both laugh and then Henry kisses me.

I guess I must have got to daydreaming for a minute there and the doctor noticed it, cause he says, "Please continue, Mrs. Quarrels."

So I tell him bout all the good years in that house, and the bad ones too, like that cold wintry day near the end of the war I was out there filling up the bird feeder, when up the Old Post Road, which was paved now, comes the Western Union truck, and I'm praying like I always did when I saw that truck on the Old Post Road, "Keep going. Please God, keep him going." But don't he stop there and give me the telegram, right under that old tree, and I sit down on one of its big old roots and read that telegram over and over like somehow if I keep doing it enough, my eyeballs passing over it will erase Henry's name off it.

That spring we had another drought, and the leaves come in all stunted and the branches had a bad case of droop. That was the saddest looking tree I ever seen. It took a very long time, but that's a strong tree with good roots, and little by little, season by season, it came back to its old self.

So I told that doctor all about the holiday picnics, the christenings, and the family reunions we held in the shade of that old friend, and about how that tree's the first thing I see out my window when I wake up in the morning and the last thing I see at night when I go out to check on the animals.

He just taking it all in, and now I'm thinking, uh-oh, and I'm starting to get scared, cause the lawyer tell me they think I'm crazy there be no trial. Just put me away somewhere, and that the end of the story. I get a trial, at least I have a chance. And I know I must be doing something wrong, cause he been smiling at me through most of it but now he not smiling, and he says, "Mrs. Quarrels, tell me what happened that morning, out by the tree." So I take a deep breath and tell him the whole sorry tale.

I tell him bout how the county want to condemn my land . . . condemn it, like they was God Almighty hisself. They talking bout condemning my land cause they want to widen the Old Post Road, let them new people get in and out of their big fancy houses, get them down to the highway so they can get to work faster. And my tree smack in the middle of things, in the way of progress.

I tell him bout all the public hearings and the court hearings I got to go to cause I tell the county I don't want their money for my land and ain't no way they gonna cut down my tree, but the county say they gonna take it anyway. And I tell the doctor how surprised I am that them new people be on my side, least ways bout the tree, cause they don't want to see it come down either. They put it in the newspaper, and take up a collection, and hire a lawyer to save my tree.

Make a long story short, the judge go ahead and condemn my land, but get the county to agree they got to use "all possible means," his exact words, to save my tree. Now the county people be all sweetness and light, cause hell, they got most of what they wanted anyway, and they tell me they gonna put a little bend in the road right there, take care of everything. So I thinking things okay now, and I get a little bit of money from the county for the land they condemned, things looking pretty good.

But then I wake up that morning and the hairs on the back of my neck standing up like a porkeypine. Something wrong. Ain't no birds, can't hear no animals. Nothing.

All of a sudden there's this god-awful roar, like the earth tearing itself apart, and I look out the window and down there by my tree there's this flat-bed truck on the Old Post Road with this giant bulldozer backing down a ramp off it. And there's these fellas out there with hard hats and big rolled-up plans and they looking at all those colored ribbons and little stakes the county put there, and I can tell from their arm motions and so on, they after my tree.

So I throw on my housecoat and go running out there but then I think, what if these fellas don't wanta listen to me, so I run back in the house and I call the lawyer and tell him to get over here, and I grab Henry's old hunting rifle and I go on over to my tree. I talk to the boss-man and he tells me he looked at the plans and it just ain't gonna work with that little bend in the road, so the tree's gotta go.

I tell him all about the judge and what he said, and he tells me the judge gave those orders to the county, and he's the State Highway Department so he ain't bound by no agreement the county made. So I ask him to wait till the lawyer come, we get this cleared up, but he tell me he can't wait. Got a schedule he gotta keep — time is money and all that. So I tell him he gonna kill this tree, he gonna have to kill me first, and meantime this bulldozer fella sitting up there on top of that monster, watching us and laughing like this the funniest thing he seen in his life. And then he get this nasty look on his face, like he looking at everything ever troubled him in his lifetime, and he yell over the sound of his engine, "Get out the way old lady, or I gonna doze you into the ground along with this old tree." And I yell back I ain't going nowhere till the lawyer get here, but don't he slam that monster into gear and come right at me with it.

"What did you do?" the doctor said.

So I answer straight-up what I done, just like the public defender told me to. "I shot the son of a bitch."

Well, I don't know what was so funny bout that, but it sure seemed to tickle that doctor. He says, "You shot him. Just that simple?"

"Simple? Wasn't nothing simple bout it. I'm shouting at him, 'Wait for the lawyer, wait for the lawyer,' but he ain't listening. He still coming, and I'm backing up, and all these things racing through my mind. . . . all them years, and my Henry, and I can't bear the thought of that tree being killed. But still he don't stop.

"And he's looking right in my eyes and I'm looking back in his and I can see there's an evil in him, cause he laughing and carrying on like maybe he's hoping I'm not going back off, like maybe killing me and this old tree just be mighty fine to him. So I close my eyes and squeeze the trigger, figuring it'll scare him off, and next thing I know the dozer stops so I'm saying, 'Thank you Lord for making him stop.'

"But something still ain't right.

"I look up there at him and he sitting there leaned back, his shoulders slumped, his hands hanging straight down past his seat, his chin resting on his chest, like he taking a nap or something, and I'm thinking, what that fool up to now? Then it hits me. Lord a mercy, I must of shot him. The foreman fella, he climbs up there, and sure enough, that dozer man dead as dead can be. Got this dead-man switch they call it, shut the dozer off soons his hands come off the controls, and that's what saved me and my tree."

The doctor gets real serious again, asks me am I sorry for what I done? Again, I answer truthful. I tell him I'm awful sorry that man be dead, but awful glad the Lord seen fit to guide that bullet, save me and my tree.

The doctor tells me our session all done, and that he'll be seeing me at the trial, which was just what I wanted to hear, so I got out of there fast, fore he could ask me any more questions.

He telephoned the other day, asks could he come out just to see how was I doing, and he'd like to see the old oak for hisself. I tell him come on out any time and we'll sit under my tree, and sip some lemonade, and I'll show him where them old initials are, and he says thanks, he'd like that very much.

AS I LOOK ACROSS THE YORK

GLORIA J. SAVAGE-EARLY

As I look across the York, a river on the Chesapeake Bay
I wonder what it would speak to me, if it could have its say

Would it tell me of the many fish it soaks from day to day
Or would it tell of a little boy that drowned one early May

As I look out across the York, a river so full of time
I think of people lost at sea, theft would be York's crime

My countenance begins to change, my happy thoughts now wane
The water brought me healing strength, that strength I must regain

As I look across the York, I search for waves of peace
I know the water can calm my soul, I pause for that release

I still myself and search within to find the peace I need
It is there within my heart, a tiny peaceful seed

As I look across the York, my tears begin to roll
Tears that have a purpose, tears that touch my soul

Tears not born from sadness rolling slowly down my cheek
Changing my thoughts to joy again, strength where I was weak

As I look across the York, I stand tall and strong again
Knowing that I can reach my goals, knowing that I will win

VAMPIRE BUNNIES IN DELTAVILLE

J.M. JOHANSEN

D eltaville, Virginia is famous as the boat building capital of the Chesapeake Bay. It became my home in 2003 when I moved into a small cottage on Lovers Lane (yes, there is a Lovers Lane). Three weeks later Hurricane Isabel hit. It was my first hurricane and my first experience with power outages. Fourteen days of power outages. I learned what a generator was, how to cook on a Coleman stove, and I got to know my neighbors. They took care of me, made sure I was okay, and made me feel safe.

I am a "come here." That means I came here from somewhere else, as opposed to a "born here" who was, well, born here. Of course, I have met people who moved to Deltaville when they were two years old, are now eighty, and are still considered a "come here." Not that it matters. The Deltavillians are my fellow citizens. In a pinch they don't care where you came from.

Deltaville is my home now. We are bordered by the Rappahannock River to the north, the Piankatank River to the south, and the Chesapeake Bay to the east. It's a quiet place to about 1,000 full-time residents. However, I know it has its secrets. Some lie on the bottom of the rivers surrounding the village. Some live on, in a rabbit cage buried in a backyard.

My neighbor Terry and her husband Claude lived in the house on my left. They were "born heres" who kept a large floppy-eared rabbit in a cage in her fenced backyard. My neighbor Edna on the other side was a "come here" who owned a chocolate lab who loved to dig under Terry's fence and knock the rabbit from his hutch. I think the lab wanted to play; the rabbit's owner didn't see it that way.

This went on for months – my neighbor on the left going off to work, the dog on the right digging under the fence and knocking the rabbit to the ground. Fussing, fighting and finally a visit from the sheriff's deputy and his accomplice, the animal control officer. "Next time we're takin' the dog and youth-a-nizing him," the animal control officer proclaimed.

"Where's McGruff?" I asked

"You mean the dog, McGruff?" the deputy asked.

"Yes. I thought maybe he could explain to Hershey why it's not nice to use rabbits as a chew toy. He speaks his language and it might help to talk with a peer. You know, take a bite outta crime."

They didn't think I was funny.

After that, Edna had a fence built, complete with a cinder block base, to insure Hershey wouldn't be able to dig his way out. She was terrified at the thought of losing her lab, so she kept him locked up in their newly secured yard. Peace and tranquility returned to our little lane in Deltaville. Hershey (the lab) and Fluffy (the rabbit) remained in their proper places.

Until one Monday morning.

Terry and Claude had gone to work. As I pulled into the driveway that separated our two houses I noticed Hershey coming out from under Terry's fence. He had Fluffy in his mouth. Both were covered with mud, and the rabbit was not moving.

I went next door, got Edna (who became hysterical at the sight of the dead rabbit). "They're going to kill Hersey! What am I going to do?" she screamed.

"I have a plan," I said. "You take Hershey home, get him cleaned up and let me tend to the rabbit."

I took the bunny into the house, plopped his lifeless body into the kitchen sink, and got the shampoo out of the bathroom. I washed him then took my hair dryer and fluffed him up. He looked great, and fortunately had no bite marks from his ill-fated encounter with Hershey.

Edna met me outside. "What's your plan?" she asked.

"My plan is to put the rabbit back in his hutch and when you-know-who comes home, there he will be – in his hutch. She'll assume he died of natural causes and all will be well once again."

We went next door, opened the gate and placed the hutch in its proper upright position. Hershey's muddy paw prints were all over the side of the hutch. I filled the rabbit's dishes with the food that had spilled out on the ground, put water in the dish and closed the door to the hutch. We left the back yard. "Keep Hershey locked up," I told Edna, my newfound I-owe-you-for-the-rest-of-my-life friend.

I cleaned up the kitchen and went to bed. I had to be at work at 11 p.m. and needed some sleep if I was going to be coherent. I got up at around 5:30 p.m. just in time to see the rabbit owner come home from work. I decided to hang around on my deck to see what happened.

Terry opened the gate, started toward the back door, stopped, and began screaming, "Fluffy! Fluffy!!" I walked from my back deck across the yard and through her open gate.

"What happened?" I asked.

"Fluffy, Fluffy," she yelled. "Fluffy!"

I walked over to the cage, looked in and said, "Oh, my goodness – I am so sorry. Poor Fluffy seems to be *el morte*!"

"I don't know who *el morte* is, but Fluffy is dead. Dead!" She seemed on the verge of hysteria.

"I am so sorry." By now the entire neighborhood was in the backyard. My neighbor across the street, who was extremely hard of hearing, asked if he needed to call the rescue squad. "No," I told him. "The rabbit has died."

"Well the rescue squad doesn't do animals," he said. "You 'come heres' are just too used to city living."

"Yes, well anyway let's get Terry here calmed down." I pulled a chair over so she could sit down before she fell down.

"You don't understand," she kept saying over and over. "You just don't understand!"

Now, I understand attachment to pets – even rabbits – but not to the extent this poor soul was exhibiting. She was sobbing, shaking, screaming Fluffy's name over and over.

Finally, she stopped, looked up, and said, "You don't understand. This morning, before I left for work, I came out to feed Fluffy."

"I do understand," I said.

"No, let me finish! He wasn't moving. He died sometime last night, I guess. So I buried him before I left for work." She pointed to the hole dug on the left side of the yard. "And now he's back in his cage like nothing happened."

I looked at my watch. "Oops, late for work!" I said as I made a hasty exit. All of the other neighbors disbanded quickly leaving Terry to tend to Resurrection Rabbit.

The rabbit's owner never figured it out. She did tell me she thought the house was haunted, started talking about vampires, a zombie apocalypse, and other things.

I certainly wasn't going to tell her the whole story…for Hershey's sake. I didn't want to see the poor dog "youth-a-nized."

She moved the next year.

Oh – and the rabbit? I think he's either buried in his cage under the tree in her backyard (the one she hung garlic on all the time) or he's lying on the bottom of the river.

Either way, Resurrection Rabbit is resting comfortably… somewhere.

THE KATY LYNN

RICHARD CORWIN

"There are three sorts of people; those who are alive, those who are dead, and those who are at sea."

- Old Capstan Chantey attributed to Anacharsis, 6th Century BC

The aged sails fell into a heap on the deck like dirty laundry. I grabbed the halyard, struggling to raise the heavy canvas. John gripped the helm in anticipation as the heap of stained, patched sail began to slowly climb the mast. Decayed leaves, pine needles, pine nuts, acorns spilled out of the rotting canvas folds and onto the deck. Remnants of a squirrels nest.

I pulled faster. Hand over hand. The sail billowed like a great parachute. New life was being breathed into the old boat; first time in many years. The *Katy Lynn* lurched, plunged forward, alive, under her own power, her bow cut deep into the murky river. She creaked, groaned then heeled over slightly. "Hooray," John yelled, "The old boat's still got some life." Chris, my date for the trip, squealed with delight.

"Let's just keep going," I yelled back to John, "make a dash for the open ocean 'til land's out of sight."

"I'll vote for that," Chris said.

"Someday," John promised, "I'll make it to the islands for some real sailing."

"Bet I'll get there before you," I yelled as I strained to

haul up the last few feet of the sail.

Then a loud, long ripping sound split the air. The fragile sail exploded into hundreds, thousands of thin slivers of decayed cloth that fluttered away in the wind like crippled birds before falling into the river. Bronze grommets from the sail clattered to the deck like old coins as empty bamboo parells, freed from the sail, rattled down the mast, finally coming to rest on the booms' yoke. The *Katy Lynn* drifted a few yards, stopped dead in the water, the wind died, a few pieces of canvas floated past, and the river once again calmly embraced the old boat. Canvas could easily be replaced.

John and I found the *Katy Lynn* when we were surveying nearby waterfront property on the York River for Steve Stephens, a local surveyor. Immediately the boat's red and white "For Sale" sign conjured up an excited discussion of fixing her up, making her sea worthy, and sailing to explore the lush islands of the Caribbean. We spent hours scanning yachting magazines, searching marinas at every opportunity, and staring at passing boats hoping that the dream would magically come alive at any minute. The *Katy Lynn* promised to be that boat. John stood on her deck, felt her strength and admired her graceful sheer. Inspired by her history and diminishing numbers he sensed she also had a strong spirit of survival. At that moment an urgency to own the old boat came over John. To give her new life; a challenge he couldn't ignore. "The *Katy Lynn*," he promised, "will make a good island boat."

* * *

In 1961 the failed Bay of Pigs invasion made headlines

as Cubans fled the Caribbean island for Miami and other northern ports. Ernest Hemmingway would not return to Finca Vigia, his beloved home in Havana. (Had he not committed suicide that summer I imagined he would more than likely have stayed to write about revolutionary Cuba.) The Berlin Wall rose almost overnight to physically divide a city, and U.S. military advisers were deployed to South Vietnam. Other than the news, it remained a pretty dull year.

Not built to be an exotic sailing ship, the *Katy Lynn* hadn't been a world traveler or explorer. As a sleek, rake-masted Chesapeake Bay Skipjack, she would never leave the bay or river tributaries during her lifetime. Half a century old, the *Katy Lynn* was built just to fish for oysters.

Sliding out of a Virginia boatyard in 1911, she proudly joined a large fleet of Skipjacks. Her white sails like a low, summer cloud fluttered across the horizon pushing her over the shallows of the bay into rich oyster beds. Once her hold was full, her crews rushed to waiting buy boats to sell their catch.

But over time pollution, disease, overfishing, smaller oysters, and destruction of oyster shell reefs would create a hardship on the oystermen. With diminishing oyster populations some traded their slower wind-dependent Skipjacks for faster, shallow draft, low-rise, diesel powered boats that could travel faster to more distant, shallower oyster beds. Others chose to give up, sell out, and retire. Some romantics refused to give up their Skipjacks, instead gave them new life, refitted, restored, and repainted as beautiful pleasure boats.

The *Katy Lynn* had a long life and many owners before

being retired. Maintenance costs had escalated dramatically with her age. With the collapse of the oyster industry her owners had little choice but tie the hapless boat to a backwater dock. There she was forgotten, neglected, stripped of her precious bronze fittings and other useable parts for salvage. The final humiliating act of her retirement was shutting and locking her hatches for good, like closing a coffin. She was ready for burial then ignored.

Years passed. Idleness took its toll. Shafts of sunlight now streaked through her hull in places where caulking had dried, rotted, fallen out. Weather beaten canvas sails were so old they had the appearance of coffee stained rags, frayed patches repaired old tears. Uneven layers of time-yellowed, cheap, white paint had blistered under the summer sun then fell away in pieces. Her untreated bleached wood looked like old bones poking out from a dead body; rusting iron fittings streaked orange tears down her hull. She was a derelict ready to be torn apart and burned.

The whine of a pump could be heard emptying the stale rainbow colored bilge water into the small marina. What began as an occasional splash became a constant flow as more caulking gave way. A heavy smell of musty wood, diesel fuel, and rejection had replaced the familiar fishy odor of oysters. The *Katy Lynn* was lost, forgotten, a home only to memories.

But, below all the visible rot and ruin, her keel remained intact – straight, solid, and in good condition: her sturdy frame of saw-cut ribs and pine decks tenaciously held her together despite the years of neglect.

John bailed her out of the watery prison and asked me to help move the boat to another marina. There he hoped to get her hauled out, re-caulked, painted, and made seaworthy once again, a project I was excited to help with. Talks of sailing the high seas, exploring Caribbean islands came to life when we stood on her deck. The islands were just around the bend in the river and the *Katy Lynn* our inspiration.

On the day of the long awaited trip, Chris, my youthful college student date, met us early at the marina with John's wife Judy. They brought a bottle of wine, a six pack of cold beer, and snacks for the trip. Judy made a quick wordless tour of the boat. John had convinced her it was a worthwhile investment before she saw it. Standing on the dock, staring at the old boat before she left, Judy shook her head as if unconvinced the *Katy Lynn* was anything more than the proverbial "hole-in-the-water."

"If you make it up river," she said almost mockingly, "I'll be there to pick you up."

At last we were ready to leave. John went to explore the engine room, check the fuel level, pump out the remaining bilge water before disconnecting the shore line, and open the water cooling valves to the engine. I began to untie a few lines, and Chris changed into an undersized bikini before climbing onto the bowsprit to watch.

John tried but failed to start the long idle engine; idle far too long to offer anything more than a loud grinding groan. One more try. With an asthmatic cough, a shudder like a death rattle, it belched a dense cloud of black smoke, quivered one more time then fell silent.

Marty, the boat's former owner, stopped by and offered to tow the *Katy Lynn* down river to her new home. Frustrated, John decided to save what little power was left in the battery and agreed. Marty tied his small outboard motorboat alongside and eased us into the narrow marshy channel and into the York River. The *Katy Lynn* was on her way to redemption.

It didn't take long, when we neared Yorktown, that we began attracting the interest of other boaters. Chris straddled the bowsprit as John and I worked on the engine. We saw several boats stop, say something to Chris, circle the boat, wave, then speed away. A couple of boats returned. As we watched, Chris leaned over the rail to grab several beers and a bag of sandwiches from one of the boats. Wondering why a stranger would come bring beer and sandwiches to her, we saw Chris fall out of her bikini top. She stood, squirmed to return her abundant breasts to her bra, and yelled thanks. The boater waved, circled again, yelled something to John and me, saluted and sped away. A few more boats stopped, some bringing beer, another one cigarettes, and some just seemed curious. Oddly most went slowly around the boat, waving, saluting, and yelling greetings. Some slowed or stopped in the water for a longer look.

Chris ran back to the engine room, gave us the cold beer, some ham and cheese sandwiches, a few cigarettes, but before we could ask what was going on, she raced back to her bowsprit perch.

The *Katy Lynn* was just an old neglected sail boat; hardly in the best of condition to attract so much interest. Although a rarely seen Skipjack, it seemed unusual to draw the attention we were getting.

"What in hell is she doing," John asked, "to get those guys to bring us all that stuff?"

"You gotta ask?" I said. "Look at her. There's more

outside of her suit than in it."

We smiled, opened another beer, lit a cigarette, and went back to the engine.

John said, "I guess two guys with beards, covered in diesel oil, on an old boat being towed down river with a girl in an overburdened bikini on board, waving at strangers, was enough to draw curious crowds."

"We are kinda different looking." I said.

Beards were not very popular in 1961. Society had accepted that only artists, actors, intellects, non-conformists, college professors, or bums wore beards.

"Who knows?" I said, "Whatever she's doing, we'll take the beer."

A few more boats passed, waved, saluted, and shouted something at us before speeding away.

* * *

Marty had untied his boat from the *Katy Lynn* so we could try her sail. After the rotted canvas exploded he came alongside and without saying a word resumed towing the Skipjack down river. We finished the last of the beer, tossed the bottles overboard, and watched them slowly disappear beneath the latte-colored water. John picked up the few grommets he could find and stuffed them into his pocket. "Still good," he said solemnly, "for a new sail."

The rest of the trip was made in disappointed silence.

The *Katy Lynn* finally reached her new home dock. Judy had been waiting impatiently to take us back to Williamsburg. After a brief discussion, about the trip, nothing more was talked about except plans for rebuilding the old boat. Crammed into Judy's Volkswagen Bug for the ride home, John remembered to ask Chris, "Why were those guys bringing us so much beer and cigarettes?"

Chris put on her cute look, smiled, and said, "I told them you had just escaped from Cuba."

* * *

Our hopes to sail to the islands ended in divorce court. John and Judy were separated within a year after the trip down the York River. John unhappily gave up the dream of sailing the *Katy Lynn* to the islands. Forced to give up the unfinished boat as part of his divorce agreement, (John thought maybe his dedication to restore the old boat was the cause of Judy's discontent), John and the *Katy Lynn* separated as well.

Chris returned to her parents' home in Bethesda, Maryland after graduating from William and Mary. Although we never saw her again she remained very much alive in our memories as did her ill-fitted bathing suit.

John eventually emerged a few years later and remarried. He and his new wife Phyllis flew to St. Thomas and bought the *Pinafore*, a Danish built sloop. I left for Florida hoping to find a boat going to the islands and eventually reunited with John in St. Thomas.

Sailing had been my dream from childhood. It began as a boy when I discovered a derelict rowboat near the Chesapeake Bay, pulled it out of the mud, patched the holes, tied a two-by-four mast to the seats, and fastened a sail made from a boat cover. Those memories returned with the *Katy Lynn*, my first real sailing adventure. That feeling of independence, smell of salt water, and friends with shared enthusiasm encouraged me. It was a feeling of fulfillment.

Although brief, that experience on board the *Katy Lynn* with John and Chris, laid the foundation for my passion and love of sailing. Three years later John and I had our own boats; living where our vision of exploring the islands had become a reality and remembering affectionately where it all began with Chris, and the *Katy Lynn* on the York River.

Several years later, on a visit to the Waterman's Museum in Yorktown, I saw an old Chesapeake Bay Skipjack permanently displayed in the park. Even though Skipjacks look pretty much the same, that one appeared to be the *Katy Lynn* with new paint and rigging. I could almost see Chris falling out of her suit, John beating on the engine, and sails ripping apart. If it was the old boat she had finally found a safe, attentive home.*

*Note: The name *Katy Lynn* is fictitious. The name of the Skipjack we sailed that day has been long forgotten. However, I did learn that Judy donated the boat. It is possible it's the one now dry docked at the museum.

THE BRIDGE

NARIELLE LIVING

"I think your grandmother is angry again."

"That's impossible, Anson." We have this conversation every month, and I always tell him the same thing. "Dead people don't get mad."

"Someone was making a ruckus in the Blue Suite last night," he said. "And with your lack of a love life, I know it wasn't you."

"Gee, thanks."

I loved Anson, I really did. To me, he was a father, grandfather, and friend all rolled into one. Plus, he was the only full time resident of my bed and breakfast, The Rose Inn Retreat, located in Yorktown, Virginia.

I'd inherited the house a few years ago from my grandmother, Sunlee, a woman who came to America in 1953 from South Korea. She used to tell me that the view of the York River and the rose gardens she'd planted made the inn a place of healing.

Anson claims my grandmother is now a *gwishin*, the Korean term for ghost. I claim that Anson is bored, having retired from a glitzy life as a newscaster, and should go out and get part time work.

"I don't know why you insist my grandmother haunts this place," I said. "What about my grandfather? He's the one who died under mysterious circumstances."

"It is clearly a female presence here," Anson stated. "Besides, I should think you'd be delighted to have her around. Ghosts draw more tourists."

Great, just what I needed, tourists who liked to be scared or were looking for a woo-woo experience.

"Have you checked with the local stations lately?" I asked, changing the subject. "Maybe WVEC news is looking for an anchor. Or WAVY."

He sniffed and looked over his half glasses at me, sipping coffee. "Caroline, dear, we've been over this before. One does not retire from working as a national evening news anchor with a major network and go on to work at a *local* station."

I turned to go back into the kitchen and get more muffins, as well as to hide my smile. Anson Peters was a very predictable man.

Or so I thought.

When I came out of the kitchen with freshly baked blueberry muffins, Anson was sitting with his arms folded on the table and a serious look on his face.

A loud thump echoed through the house. "I told you she had something to say," he said. "I think your grandmother knows what I'm going to talk to you about."

My heart dropped to my stomach. *Please don't tell me you're moving. Please.* For the past three years I'd come to rely on not only his steady rent, but also his friendship.

I did not want to lose Anson.

"I'm not leaving," he said.

"I didn't — "

"I can tell from the look on your face that's what you were thinking," he said. "No, this is bigger than that. It's why your gwishin grandmother has been active."

Bigger than Anson moving? I shuddered, not liking where this conversation was going.

"As you know, I've spent some of my free time researching the history of this area," he said.

Anson had an obsession with history, which was why he loved living here. For him, it was perfect; he got to live in an old house, surrounded by antiques, without any of the responsibility of maintenance, taxes, or having to cook for himself. It was a win-win situation for both of us.

"I've begun delving into your family history," he continued.

"We're not very interesting," I said.

Anson shook his head. "Yes, you are. Imagine your grandmother as a war bride, arriving at this huge house that belonged to her husband's family, a scared and lonely young woman trying to build a new life."

My grandmother never struck me as scared of anything. I always knew her to be a strong, determined person, a champion of justice. I remember the time she marched down to the county administrator's office to give him a piece of her mind about some new ordinance or other he was trying to pass.

The ordinance was not passed.

"She might have been lonely, Anson, I'll give you that. I don't know about scared, though."

"Of course she was scared, especially after your grandfather died."

My grandfather's death was still a mystery to me. My mother told me he died when she was only seven years old. The only pictures I had of him showed a handsome young man in his Army uniform.

"Haven't you ever wondered why your mother and grandmother never spoke of him?" Anson asked.

"Of course I wondered, but I wasn't comfortable prying," I answered. The one time I'd tried to get any answers from my mother she'd refused to discuss the matter.

"There's no easy way to say this," Anson began. "But I found your grandfather's death certificate, and it lists his cause of death."

My heart rate increased. Finally, an answer to my question. Why hadn't I thought to look there?

"It was self-inflicted." Anson's words hung in the air.

"What do you mean, self-inflicted? He killed himself?"

Anson nodded. "I'm sorry."

The years of secrecy suddenly made sense. Suicide carried shame and left a family burdened with a multitude of what-ifs.

"There's more. I've been looking through the old registration books," he said. Months ago, Anson had asked if he could go through the ledgers, looking at decades of guest sign-ins. I didn't see the harm, so of course I agreed.

"I noticed some of the names have a notation, 'referred by Sharon.' It looks like Sharon has been referring people here for years."

"I still get those calls, but not as many as when my grandmother was alive," I said. "She used to harp on me to be sure I wrote it in the book." I paused, watching Anson. "What does this have to do with my grandfather?"

For the first time since I'd known him, Anson looked uncomfortable. "I'm not certain," he said. "Let's wait until tomorrow to see if I'm correct."

"What's tomorrow?"

"You have a guest arriving," he said.

"That's right," I said, remembering taking the

reservation. "He was referred here by Sharon."

"Do you know Sharon?" Anson asked.

I shook my head. "No, I always assumed it was someone who knew my grandmother, especially since she was so careful about recording the name. This is the first time since I've taken over the inn that a referral from Sharon hasn't cancelled. Once they find out grandma isn't here, they don't make the reservation."

He nodded. "I think your new guest is the reason your grandmother was distressed. She's trying to tell us something."

"Anson, how many times do I have to tell you, my grandmother has moved on to the great beyond and is not haunting The Rose Inn Retreat?"

Another thump sounded overhead.

He reached over and patted my hand. "I know you're not ready yet, my dear, but try to open your mind a bit. Remember, it's my job to get to the bottom of the story, and there's definitely a story in this house."

* * *

I didn't sleep well that night. Was there really a story about this house? Why had my grandmother never discussed her life in Korea? And, most importantly, who the heck was Sharon?

The warm April morning was dark, with clouds obscuring the sunlight and rain pelting my roof. Check-in time is 2 p.m., so I kept busy until my mystery guest arrived.

At exactly 2:05 an older gentleman came through the front door as if he'd lived here all his life. He looked to be in his seventies and wore a raincoat and fedora. He smiled when he saw me behind the front desk.

"Caroline?" he said, approaching the desk. "I called last week about a reservation."

I pretended to consult the book, despite the fact that I knew darn well what it said. "You must be Will," I said. "You'll be in the Blue Room, as requested."

He gave me a sad smile. "Perfect. That used to be your grandmother's favorite room."

I hadn't expected that. "Did you know my grandmother well?"

He nodded. "I should make time to visit more often, but... life gets in the way."

I had to ask. "And Sharon? How do you know Sharon?"

Will's gaze assessed me, not unkindly. "Let me get my luggage, then we can retire to the library. Perhaps it's time we talked."

I called Anson in his room and told him to join us. I knew he would want to hear whatever Will had to say, plus I wanted him with me for support. Minutes later, the three of us gathered around the polished mahogany table in the library. Will's voice was soft with age, and his words were hesitant. "I first met your grandmother at No Gun Ri in July of 1950."

I could hear Anson's sharp intake of breath. "The bridge."

Will nodded. "Sunlee was a remarkable woman, a unique combination of determination and compassion. That day, she was escaping North Korea, trying to find her way to freedom."

"How did she manage to survive that atrocity?" Anson asked.

I was embarrassed, but I had to say something. "I'm sorry, I don't really know what No Gun... I don't know what you're talking about."

Anson turned to me. "No Gun Ri is a village in South Korea, a place refugees flooded during the war to escape North Korea. The United States Army massacred civilians at the stone bridge there."

"You have to understand how it really happened," Will said. "The North Koreans were incredibly brutal to prisoners of war as well as their own civilians, beyond anything we'd ever seen before. We were told that refugees from North Korea were probably spies and would kill us, and at that point we'd seen enough to know the cruelties they were capable of. Our orders were to shoot anyone crossing the border."

Tears appeared in the corners of Will's eyes, and I could see the tremor in his hands. "It was the worst thing I've ever been in," he whispered. "People were screaming all around me... the Koreans were scrambling to hide, digging holes in the sand to escape our attack." Will stopped, taking a deep breath. "Your grandmother survived that battle by stacking and hiding behind dead bodies."

The enormity of Will's description left me breathless. "She never talked about any of this," I said. "Whenever I asked about her life in Korea she broke down and cried, so I stopped asking."

Will shook his head. "Your grandmother was amazing. She knew what the leaders in her country were capable of, and she devoted herself to working with the American forces in any way she could."

"Was she a spy?" Anson asked.

Will smiled. "She might have helped with a couple of missions."

"It's probably not classified information anymore," Anson said.

Will shook his head. "I'd rather not discuss it. But I will tell you that even after the war ended she continued to help us."

A memory surfaced in my mind. "I remember the groups that used to meet in the library," I said. "Groups of older men, soldiers. I wasn't allowed to interrupt the meetings."

"We all had some sort of post traumatic stress disorder, PTSD. Your grandmother provided a refuge for us, a place we could talk without fear of being judged. I think your grandfather was forever grateful for that."

My grandmother had dedicated her life to helping veterans, maybe even the ones who had orders to kill her all those years ago.

"Did my grandparents meet at… that place?" I asked.

Will nodded. "Ironic, right? The place he was supposed to kill her, instead he fell in love with her. He saw her running and disobeyed orders to shoot. He told me he never knew what made him hesitate, but before he realized what he was doing he ran out, met her at the bridge, and dragged her to safety."

"That doesn't make sense," I said. "If he loved her so much, why'd he go and kill himself and leave her and my mother behind?"

Anson cleared his throat. "I've never personally been in combat, but I've covered enough stories in war zones overseas to know that sometimes there's no escaping the nightmare of battle."

"We all wanted to do what your grandfather did," Will said. His gaze on me was direct and unblinking. "I used to think about taking my life every day. But I was lucky, and with help I got through it."

It was easy to imagine my grandmother opening the doors of her home to veterans seeking solace, providing a day or a week to absorb the peace of the river. She had created a retreat at the house, a perfect place for healing.

"I have one more question," I said. "Who is Sharon?"

Thump. Clearly, Anson was right. My grandmother was listening.

Will smiled. "That's your grandmother's sense of humor."

"Let me guess," Anson said. "The Rose of Sharon, right?"

Will nodded. "Yes. The Korean national flower is the Rose of Sharon. Anytime we made a reservation here that was the code we used to let your grandmother know we were a veteran, and she'd set up the meetings."

Will stood and looked at us. "It's getting late, and I'm rather tired. I think it's time for me to go to my room and rest a bit."

I had to ask one more question. "Why do you request the Blue Room each time you stay here?"

"To be close to your grandmother," he answered.

When he left the room I remained seated next to Anson, lost in my thoughts.

"You're going to do the same thing, aren't you?" he asked.

I nodded. "It's the right thing to do. Maybe I can arrange a more formal sort of thing, bring in a counselor or someone to help facilitate groups for veterans."

I would find a way to carry on the tradition of healing.

"She's going to like this," he said.

Thump.

"I'm sure she will," I said.

SAILING, APRIL

JULIE LEVERENZ

We fill the tanks, find the charts,
stash the food, the sheets, the clothes,
lock the car, use the head,
start the engine,
cast off.

A deadrise churns the narrow Cut,
swirly *Susan Janes* astride her bow.
We give way — streaming bubbles curve astern.
The rubber-coveralled captain nods,
knee-deep in oysters.

Only tiny riffles; the sails stay furled.
The engine growls, spits watery exhaust,
skirting channel markers, shiny on tarry posts
topped by precarious stick-jumbles
and shrieking Osprey.

At the bridge our tall mast slices through
the dimness below and hurry-hurry above
of thundering shadows and bright sun flashes,
leaving get-ready-go hassles behind
for carefree waters ahead.

A blue tub-toy boat patrols the Shipyard shore,
dwarfed by crane and aircraft carrier.
Smooth waves fan out from a sand-laden barge
tugged down from Richmond.
Anchored container ships ride high.

A halyard slaps, the wind comes up.
Hoist the sails: reach, pull, cleat, repeat;
the jib and main flap and fill.
I cut the engine.
Quiet.

He takes the helm, I stretch out at the bow,
propped on a cushion, shaded by the sail.
Lapping waves shush by below;
sea-salty breeze ruffles our hair.
We exhale.

HEADLIGHTS IN THE REARVIEW

GREG LILLY

"**D**id you see this?" Claire slapped the newspaper on the breakfast table in front of her husband. "A murder – on the Colonial Parkway. That's not ten minutes from here."

Frank's hand trembled as he placed his coffee down, rattling the cup against the oak tabletop.

He scanned the article as Claire stood by the counter and watched him. The news had startled her, but now as she saw Frank's reaction, she regretted being so abrupt. She knew he worried about the murders starting up again. Even when they had dated, Frank avoided driving on the parkway after dark. He claimed it was because of the possibility of hitting a deer, but Claire knew the rumors and whispers had left him jittery of headlights in his rearview mirror.

"Geez," he said with an air of detachment. "Everyone will say the Parkway Killer is back. It's probably some copycat nutcase."

His wide, unblinking eyes didn't convince Claire of his indifference. "I know it's a scary possibility," she said, hoping to soothe him, "and the FBI had said the killer was probably dead by now. You're right. The guy must be some crazy mimic. The police will catch him… I mean with DNA testing and all that science stuff they show on television, how can they not?"

A sip of his coffee seemed to focus his mind; the mild hazelnut aroma of the creamer enticed Claire to refill her own cup. "That was a bad time," he began. "Dad and Mom were having problems. She suspected another woman. I was still in high school and spent all my free time with friends." He picked up his coffee, brought it to his lips, but set it back down without drinking. "The Parkway Killer started shooting people. All of us on the football team would kid each other about the killer following us in his car. Rumor was the car was a black Oldsmobile Toronado – you know it had that long hood and was heavy as shit. Stephen King's *Christine*, about the demon car, had come out a few years earlier, so we all thought the car was more menacing than the man."

Claire sat down at the table and rubbed the back of his hand that rested on the newspaper. He stared at his coffee cup with Tech's VT logo.

"After I left for Virginia Tech," he continued, "the murders still popped up. The last was in 1989."

"On a better subject," Claire said, "I'm going by your parents' house after work to help your mom choose wallpaper for the guest bathroom. She says your father has no opinion."

"That house is too big for them." Frank stood and dumped his remaining coffee into the sink then placed his cup in the dishwasher. "But, I'm glad they're back close to us. Mom says that Navy families always have a lot of visitors, that's why she needs the big house."

* * *

Claire left her job off Route 5 and drove across to Jamestown Road. Without thinking, she used the Colonial Parkway as a shortcut to her in-laws' house in Kingsmill. The winter white of the sky darkened as she drove along the James River, waves choppy from the wind.

Her father-in-law was always distant, as if being a Navy officer had made him superior to those around him. His career took him and his wife Sandra all over the world. They had lived the longest in Williamsburg while Frank grew up, but moved in 1990, a couple of years after Frank left for college.

She thought of Frank's comment about the Parkway Killer again: "The last was in 1989."

The theories on the unsolved murders ran the spectrum, from a serial killer catching young lovers on dark pull-outs along the Parkway to a law enforcement officer gone rogue and killing for the fun of it. Consensus said the predator won the trust of the victims since there was never a sign of struggle and usually the car window was down, as if someone of authority had tapped on the glass to start a conversation. The resulting scenes were anything but conversational. Gun blasts. Massacres.

Claire released her tight grip on the steering wheel, flexing her fingers to bring back the circulation. *Just a coincidence that Frank's parents had left town then.* Her thoughts swarmed around Earl. He had been a good father to Frank and a great husband to Sandra. *But...* How could she think that? She dismissed the accusation. *Could Earl do such a thing?* Maybe the shifty eyes, as if he was always on alert. Maybe the lean and rigid posture, as if he kept his body ready for a fight. Maybe his family outings to the shooting range, as if they were a private militia.

"Come on, Claire," she scolded herself. "This is your father-in-law of twenty years." Yet, the doubts shadowed her as she drove away from the James River and into the woods around Halfway Creek. Headlights appeared in her rearview, about 200 yards back. She didn't remember noticing a car behind her. She increased her speed until she saw the exit to Highway 199. Merging her Camry into the evening traffic felt like amnesty.

* * *

"Where's Earl?" Claire asked her mother-in-law as they flipped through books of wallpaper samples.

"Who knows? That man is always out golfing, drinking with his friends, attending civic groups. If I didn't know better, I'd say he has a girlfriend." Sandra took a deep breath and poured them both more wine. Her silver hair held a short bob with bangs that gave an easy-going vibe which offset her husband's strict crew-cut hair and personality. "Of course, Earl still presents a handsome figure. I could see how a girl could be swayed. I was." She winked at Claire.

"He's a handsome man. That's where Frank gets his looks," Claire said.

"Frank and his dad are so much alike. Really, they were best friends as Frank grew up. It's good to be back here close to him – and you, of course."

Sandra's finger traced the curve of a vine pattern on a sample. "Earl's out again tonight. I thought he was going over to your house to see Frank."

"No, I'm here," Earl's voice thundered as he slammed the garage door on the other side of the kitchen. "Just getting a few things before heading out again." He swung a gym bag in his right hand as he leaned over to kiss the top of his wife's head. To Claire's surprise, he did the same to her when he passed by – an abnormal act of affection from him. "How're my two favorite girls?"

"Good," Claire managed to say before he disappeared to the other end of the house.

"Earl," Sandra called, "will you be home for dinner?"

His voice boomed back, "The guys are meeting at the club tonight. I'll probably eat there."

The comment didn't produce a reaction from Sandra, all she said was: "Whatever." Maybe, Claire thought, after all these years, missing dinner together didn't matter.

Then Sandra switched subjects, pushing the wallpaper book toward Claire. "What do you think of this sample? The ivy isn't too dominant or overpowering?"

Overpowering. The word triggered Claire's memory. "Did you hear about the murder on the Colonial Parkway?" Claire asked in a whisper. "Back in the late '80s, they thought the Parkway Killer might be more than one person. You know since he killed young couples, one man with a gun couldn't walk up on two people, but if he partnered with another man to ambush..." Her mind went numb.

She couldn't focus on what Sandra said in response, something about *marriage towels* or more likely *marriage vows.* Claire tried organizing her thoughts: Two men, needing secrecy sworn about what they did, about their sins – the sins of the father... paid for by the son.

Earl and Sandra moved after Frank left for college, but he and Earl would have been back together on breaks and during the summer. Frank craved his father's approval. Earl gave it so seldom. She had witnessed Frank's joy when Earl tossed it his way. Even worse than suspecting her father-in-law was suspecting her own husband. She stood from the table and walked into Sandra's kitchen to clear her head.

Still with the gym bag in his hand, Earl rushed by and out the side door. "Got people to see and things to do…" his voice faded into the garage as his Mercedes SUV cranked up and backed out.

"You okay, Claire?" Sandra called from the dining room. "You're working too hard at that job of yours. You're away from home as much as Earl."

"Yes, I'm fine," she said, tensing her shoulders then forcing out the tightness with a shudder. "I just need to get to the house."

Sandra walked her to the front door. "Now, don't you worry about those stories about crazy men. The only things that make men crazy are the women in their lives." She laughed as if they shared a secret.

The Camry's engine idled while Claire sat in the driveway of her in-laws' house. She called Frank. "Where are you?" she asked, a bit more intense than she wanted to sound.

"Home. You still at Mom's?"

"Yes. Have you seen your father tonight?"

"No. Why do you ask?"

She hesitated.

"Claire, what's wrong?"

An island of desperation, that's how she felt. She should have been able to talk to Frank about anything, but this was his father and – she hated admitting – it was about him, too. "I'm on my way home." She wanted to see him face-to-face.

* * *

Frank paced as she walked in. "You've got that look I know too well," he said and stopped in front of her, concern wrinkling his forehead. "You don't want to say it, but you suspect Dad of that murder."

Relief, at least part relief, sprayed over her like the small whitecaps she'd seen on the James. "I don't –" she stopped then tried again, "I do. But why do you think that?"

"Geez, I had the same thoughts for years. I've seen this wild look in his eyes, especially back then. He acted like a caged animal. I thought it was an affair, like Mom did."

"You're not involved in anything he's up to?"

"Me? No." His face lost expression. "You thought... Claire?"

"I thought it had been two people. The murders stopped when your parents went to California after you left for Tech. Now, your dad retires and moves back here. A murder happens on the parkway, same as before: a couple pulled off after dark. Both shot through the head." Her stomach cramped at saying the words out loud.

"No, not me. I could never."

She wrapped her arms around him. "I know that. I was unnerved." The thought hit her first as a brilliant idea then as stupid. She decided to go with her first impulse. "Let's drive down the parkway. Your dad is out somewhere tonight. I mean, really if it could possibly be him, we could talk some sense into him."

Frank – large as a doorway, but less open – shook his head in a dull rejection of the idea. "Are you crazy?"

"Think about it. There are two of us. Just what the

predator wants. We park at a pull-out by the river and wait."

"What if we're totally off? It's not Dad; it's some crazed psycho. We'll be dead."

"The difference is," she reasoned, "we are expecting it. We're on guard. We have our cell phones ready and a foot on the gas pedal."

* * *

"This is insane," Frank repeated the mantra as Claire drove the dark road along the James River.

She saw no headlights behind them. Tension trembled her body, and she hoped Frank didn't notice since this idea had been hers. She pulled into a parking area that usually had a view of the river, but fog had rolled in.

A car drove past them and disappeared into the mist.

They looked at each other.

"Did you see what type of car that was?" Frank asked.

"Big. Dark. Some type of SUV."

Headlights pricked the haze down the road; the right one on high-beam. Claire started the engine and pulled onto the parkway before the car came closer. It followed them. "Call your dad," she said. "See if he's in his car."

He punched the display panel on the car to call through Claire's cell phone.

Earl's deep voice rumbled through the car speakers, "This is Earl."

"Dad," Frank spoke toward the microphone. "Where are you?"

"Just pulling into the driveway. You coming over? Sounds like you're in the car."

Claire sped up as the headlights moved closer, the right

one almost blinding her.

"No, we're heading into town," Frank said. "Didn't know what you and Mom were doing for dinner."

"Hell if I know. Probably on my own. You mother's Range Rover isn't here. I told her not to drive at night until I got that headlight fixed. One's stuck on bright. I think she knocked it out of line. "

The rearview mirror flashed white. The car jerked Claire as it was bumped from behind.

SCATTERED SECRETS

DAVID J. CARR

The paramedic did a double take when I pulled a Medicare card from my jacket pocket and handed it to her. "Yes. It's mine. I'm Janice Marsalis." Her surprise at the card should have bolstered my ego. But not today. My ego was trapped in the charred remains of the Ultra Light, lying upside down at the south end of the parking lot at Kingsgate Shopping Center, where it had crashed about forty-five minutes earlier.

When I saw the woman who pulled me from the wreck moments before the gas tank exploded being questioned by the police, reality set in. I reached for the smart phone, which I carried in the zippered pocket with my insurance cards. Williamsburg Attorney Martin Bader had settled my mother's estate only a week ago and his number was still on my speed-dial. "It's Janice," I began, pressing the phone close to block out the commotion around me. "I've had an accident. No, not in the car, the Ultra Light."

"Good God! Are you hurt?" Martin asked.

"Just bruises and a few minor burns. I'm simply thankful that no one else was injured. But I need you here. The police are waiting for the EMT people to finish before they interview me. And, I could use a ride back to the Gloucester airport to get my car when they're done." Shaken and feeling incredibly stupid, I told Martin where I was and ended the call. He was on his way.

Before the crash site was cordoned off, curious shoppers had converged upon the wreck like a flock of hungry gulls, trampling the stark white ash that led back to the plane's initial point of impact. Lilly would probably be laughing about that.

A few hours later, the interviews over, Martin and I headed to Gloucester. As we entered the Colonial Parkway, he began the familiar lecture, but with more fervor. "You know you'll probably lose your pilot's license over this, don't you? A woman seventy-three years old has no business flying. What in God's name were you thinking, flying so low over a shopping center?"

"Not now, Martin, it's complicated. If you're free tomorrow morning at nine, I'll explain everything. I certainly won't be attending my morning Zumba class."

Martin gave a reluctant nod. "Fine."

"But do get me the name of the woman who pulled me from the wreck. The police have it. I need to thank her for saving my life." Emotionally and physically spent, I slouched back, shut my eyes, and massaged my shoulder, which still ached from hanging upside down in the safety harness. How could Martin be so self-righteous about the chain of events that he put in motion? I'd have to set him straight on that.

When I got home, exhausted but too disturbed to sleep, I sat down at the kitchen table and picked up the sealed envelope he gave me last Monday at the reading of Mother's will.

I had left his office that day and hurried to my car to open it. Inside I found a key and a letter from my late mother, written three years earlier on her ninetieth birthday. Shockwaves rippled through my body as I mentally digested the first paragraph. Good God! I not only was adopted;

I was illegitimate. My biological mother was Mother's sister, my Aunt Lilly; the black sheep of the family who everybody said was crazy. I knew Lilly had died in a private sanatorium in 1940, but assumed it was because she was mentally ill. The letter made it clear that my grandparents sent her there to save them the humiliation of having to explain their unmarried daughter's pregnancy. I couldn't believe it. Seventy-three years had passed. Why had I never been told?

Feelings of anger and betrayal gave way to obsession as I continued reading. Aunt Lilly's journal, mostly written while she was in the sanatorium, was locked in a small trunk hidden in the attic at Mother's house, the Gloucester Point property I officially inherited minutes earlier. I needed to get that journal.

My mind reeled as I sped across the York River into Gloucester County. I always wondered why I was so different. Not anything like my family, preoccupied as they were with proper etiquette and social status. I hated their stodgy dinner parties, where I would be forced to wear prissy evening gowns and make small talk with people culturally programmed for little else. Mother made no effort to hide her disapproval when I refused to attend them after turning twenty-one. Like Aunt Lilly, I was a misfit, a rebel.

When I reached the house, I raced to the attic, key in hand, and found the trunk. Inside were the journal and a small wooden box about six inches square. I took both downstairs to the study, where I sat for the rest of the evening devouring Lilly's handwritten memories.

I saw much of myself in Lilly, similar passions and

contempt for social convention. Like me, she loved flying. Tucked under the front cover was her license issued in 1934, along with her degree from the College of William and Mary's Department of Aeronautics. Early journal entries recounted how she had fallen in love with another student pilot and, despite the family's protests, moved in with him — unmarried. Disowned by the family, the couple borrowed $300 from friends, bought one of the then defunct flight school's aircraft, a Fleet Trainer, and started a crop dusting business. With the depression taking its toll, they picked up extra money, taking wealthy tourists for sightseeing flights over the area. Lilly told of their big break in 1939 when they won a contract to spot menhaden for the Reedville fishing fleet.

All was going well until the entries beginning in June 1939. Lilly discovered she was pregnant. Her partner, apparently unable to face the realities of marriage and fatherhood, had abandoned her and joined the Army Air Corps. Left to run the business alone, and with no family support, her usually impeccable prose in the journal became choppy, signs of deepening depression cropping up on every page. Her last entry before a break of fifteen calendar days noted that she was headed out on a routine flight to spot menhaden. She worried about money, knowing her pregnancy would soon make it impossible to fly.

Stowed in between the empty pages were a number of local newspaper clippings detailing her crash at sea. The plane was never recovered, but she was found unconscious the next morning on the shores of Tangier Island. According to the news reports, Lilly spotted a large school of menhaden in the middle of the bay. At the edge of the school she saw something large, something she'd never seen before. It was circling the menhaden, herding them into a smaller, denser circle. Flying low to determine what it could be, a sudden burst of wind flipped the plane, sending it nose first into the menhaden school.

According to the newspaper accounts, Lilly surfaced, searching for some wreckage to keep her afloat, but there was none. Treading water, she claimed to have felt something under the surface gently nudging her abdomen, vibrating. Terrified it was a shark, she instinctively reached down only to feel the water swirl about her as whatever it was abruptly pulled back. Minutes passed with no further contact. Weak and succumbing to the cold water, she sank into a semi-conscious state and slipped beneath the surface. The news reporters had asked her to explain how she reached Tangier Island, miles away. She hesitated. "A miracle, a mysterious miracle," she said. "You would think me insane if I told you, and I'm not sure I believe it myself. Maybe I was dreaming. Let's leave it at that."

Who or what saved her — and me, the unborn child in her womb? I flipped past the blank pages of the journal, hoping to find the answer. Then I saw the long entry that, in the letter Martin had given me, Mother had referred to as preposterous. The entry was written the week after Lilly was admitted to the sanatorium.

I dare not tell anyone the real story of my rescue for fear of being judged insane and kept in this place forever, but I offer it here.

As I sank below the surface for what I believed to

be the last time, I felt something big rising up between my dangling legs, pushing me to the surface, then above it. I instinctively leaned forward, wrapping my arms about it to keep from falling off, like I used to do when riding bareback on the pony Father gave me on my twelfth birthday.

It began to move forward, slowly at first. Then, it picked up speed. Every now and then its head would break the surface about three yards in front of me. Shaped like a football, its head was no wider than its eel-shaped torso to which I clung for dear life. Was this what I had seen herding the menhaden before I crashed?

The sun had set and there was no moonlight. I was about to lose my grip when the stinging sensation of marsh grasses lashed my numbed arms and legs. Split seconds later, my hold was broken as my rescuer abruptly reversed direction, catapulting me over its head into the reeds. Chaotic splashing from behind sprayed mud all over me. By the time I turned to see, whatever it was had disappeared back into the bay. I was ashore. I didn't care.

But Lilly did care. Every journal entry for weeks afterward added bits to the story. In the sanatorium library, she did research, trying to reconcile what had happened with reality. Her doctors questioned her emotional stability, but she wouldn't give up. The last entry was one of excitement. In 1933, there had been a confirmed sighting of a reptilian oddity termed a "dragon" on the Patuxent River in Maryland. Lilly became convinced that this was the creature that had saved her. She believed it did so because she was carrying a child, and somehow it had detected the baby in her womb with its gentle nudging of her abdomen. Its instinct to protect the unborn was responsible for it acting to save her. It was not a monster, but a caring creature, perhaps itself a mother. She had named it "Chessie," to this day the name used to describe similar sightings of the creature.

Closing the journal, I turned my attention to the cardboard box. Glued to it was an age-yellowed, note-size envelope from the sanatorium. It was addressed "To Lilly's heirs." Obviously no one had ever opened it. Even in death, Lilly remained disowned by the family. But no more, I thought as I carefully peeled it from the box.

The envelope contained a note in Lilly's handwriting, apparently written on her deathbed. The note asked that her ashes be spread from a plane over the runway of Scott Airport in Williamsburg, where she had learned to fly. Her journal entries told of the thrill when she met Amelia Earhart there in 1933.

I'd stared at the box. "My God! It's Lilly's ashes!" Her last wishes had not been honored. I vowed to correct that. Better seventy-three years late than never. But Scott Airport? Where was that? It had taken me a few days to figure that out.

The next morning, after putting fresh bandages on my burns, I drove to Martin's office. I decided the best strategy was to walk him through the past week's discoveries. He would have many questions, the first of which would be why I was flying over Kingsgate Shopping Center. That was the easy one. The shopping center was built on the site of Scott Airport, the place in 1934 where Lilly had received her pilot's training.

Few people alive know of the College of William and Mary's short-lived flight school or its airport at Scott Field, but by the end of our meeting, Martin Bader would be one of them. We talked for an hour. When I told him the story about my real mother and how she was saved, his eyes widened in disbelief. But it didn't matter. I believed it. The legal issues fully discussed, I thanked him. As I got up to leave, he handed me an envelope.

"Yesterday you asked me to get more information about the woman who pulled you from the burning wreckage," Martin said. "Well, here it is."

I pocketed the envelope and drove to Kingsgate Shopping Center. I wanted to spend one last moment with my true mother. The remains of the Ultra Light had been removed, but traces of Lilly's ashes were still visible on the parking lot. I smiled. She was finally at rest, scattered secrets exposed. I reached in my pocket and pulled out the envelope Martin had given me. When I saw the name he'd written on the index card inside, I gasped. Chessie! Chessie DePaul — my "Chessie." I knew what Lilly would say.

Sunrise on the Bay

Carol J. Bova

She left the tiny cottage before dawn, easing the screen door closed so it wouldn't bang. The row of summer houses felt closer than they were, but sounds echoed in the quiet hours of darkness. Darcy rented out her cottage every summer, keeping four weeks overlapping April and May for herself. She hurried down to the beach that gave her a view she loved for her sunrise photography.

A soft breeze caressed her cheek, and she closed her eyes remembering a moment years earlier before looking upward. Watching the sky lighten brought her a feeling of soaring, like one of the sea birds taking off from the marsh to glide over the waves. Colors reflected and expanded on the waters of the bay, changing second by second. Today would be a pink and lavender morning if the first hints came true. These mornings were Darcy's favorites — abstract pools of color blending and merging on slow waves. Clouds stretched along the horizon filtered the emerging light into fans, spreading above and below its still hidden source. Darcy moved along, crouching down, aiming upward at different angles to catch more, then less of the beach grasses in the foreground. As if responding to every click of the camera's shutter, the sky shifted, growing lighter, shade by shade, until yellow light leapt into morning.

Darcy packed up her cameras, feeling alone and exposed next to the crashing surf as the tide turned. Shivering from the chilly breeze off the water, she jogged back to her battered Land Rover and drove to Lynne's Restaurant on

Route 198. Bits of local conversations about kids, work, and weather flew around the room while she ate her bacon and eggs. She felt curious eyes on her now and then.

"Anything else?"

"Just a coffee to go, please."

She paid the check and stepped outside. No abstract colors now, not even clouds to break up the blue sky. Darcy shook off a sense of loss and decided to drive to Newport News to deliver prints to the museum gift shop. *Might as well take care of business and get it out of the way.*

She unlocked a steel storage case to double-check that the prints were in their waterproof box — she couldn't trust her memory these days. The last time she forgot to check cost her two days driving to pick up prints and get back in time for a gallery opening. Satisfied they were all there, she folded her map so the route was on the outer fold and drove off. She spotted an eagle and wished she didn't have to go to the city. Blinking lights on the highway alert message board just ahead caught her attention, and Darcy pulled into a parking lot to dial 511 and check traffic information.

"Coleman Bridge," she told the automated service and received a report of a scheduled bridge opening in forty minutes. "I should be able to make it," she said under her breath, "but no time for eagle watching." She caught herself going five or ten miles over the limit several times and slowed down. She wasn't fond of sitting at an opened bridge, but speeding tickets were worse.

Traffic was kind, and she reached the bridge well in advance of the lift. With that worry out of the way, she smiled at sailboats on the choppy water and gulls floating on currents next to the bridge. A few miles later, she picked up the interstate and was soon at the museum. The paperwork took only a few minutes before she was on the way to the nearby Mariners Museum Park.

After parking near an entrance to the Noland Trail, which wound around the park, she transferred her coffee to an insulated container and put it into an outer pocket of her backpack. She slung the strap of her favorite camera around her neck and shrugged on the pack, breathing in the clean outdoor scent before setting out along the trail. Every turn gave her opportunities for pictures of trees or water or wooden footbridges. Halfway around, she stopped at a picnic area to enjoy the bird sounds and sip her coffee.

A runner coming up the trail called out, "Keep an eye on the clouds. Storm's on the way."

"Thanks. Appreciate the info." Darcy knew how fast the weather could change and was annoyed with herself for not checking the weather report today. Rain wasn't a problem — her backpack had waterproofed compartments. Lightning near water and trees was another story. She made it back to the Land Rover just as the wind strengthened, and the sky darkened. She pulled out the weather radio, fiddling with it until she finally hit the NOAA weather channel.

Darcy recognized the serious weather intonations of the familiar synthesized male voice and turned up the volume. "Doppler radar indicated a line of strong thunderstorms capable of producing winds to forty knots. Mariners can expect gusty winds, high waves, dangerous lightning. Boaters should seek safe harbor immediately until this storm passes."

By the time Darcy reached the bridge, rain hammered against the windshield. As the sky grew even darker, a creeping sense of dread increased. When she reached the Gwynn's Island Bridge, gusts of wind pushed her toward the guardrail, and rain came down in sheets. Halfway across, Darcy stared in horror as a large waterspout formed just to the side of the bridge. She pushed as fast as she dared to reach the other side, but the capricious winds turned and moved away from the bridge toward Mathews Courthouse. As she reached the cottage, a bolt struck a tree next door. The thunderclap was immediate, and her hands shook trying to get the door unlocked. A second and third strike hit nearby. Darcy grabbed her sleeping bag off the camp cot and dragged it into the empty pantry. She dropped her camera on it and ran back for her emergency sack, a blanket, pillow, and jug of water.

She pulled the weather radio from the camera bag and between crackling noises, heard tornado warnings. Once she'd turned on the battery-powered lantern from her emergency sack, she slammed the pantry door closed.

The current tornado warning expired, and the tornado watch that replaced it lasted for the next five hours. There was nothing to do now but wait, curled up on the blanket with the sleeping bag over her for protection. With the wailing winds outside, flashes from lightning spilling under the bottom of the pantry door and the constant thunder, she had no defense against remembering her trip to Newport News fifteen years earlier.

Lightning had lit up the sky from three directions at once. Thunderclaps so loud, they'd rattled the windows in the Land Rover, and she'd slammed into walls of rain while the wind pushed her toward the ditch. Gritting her teeth and holding tight to the steering wheel for another thirty miles, she'd pulled into the hotel lot and called Robert.

"Hi there. Where are you?" Concern filled his voice.

"Downstairs in the lot."

"Have much trouble with the storms?"

"Only ran into two of them, but they slowed me down. Sorry I'm so late."

"That's okay. I'm glad you're here safe. Tired?"

"Oh yeah. Six hundred miles and only two quick stops for gas and coffee."

"Come on up so you can get to bed. My room's on the second floor, last one on the left."

When Darcy reached the room, she tapped on the door. Robert opened it and lifted her off the ground in a tight hug before the door could swing closed.

She laughed. "Could we at least close the door first?"

"If you insist." He put her down and kissed her on the forehead before locking the door, then wrapped his arms around her and kissed her until she was breathless.

She pulled back to look up at his face and smiled when he nodded his head toward the bed. He kissed her hair and along her neck. "You must be tired."

"Yeah, I guess I am. How early do you have to leave?" She began unbuttoning his shirt.

"Have a nine o'clock flight, so I need to leave here before six."

"Guess we'd better get to bed then."

In the morning, they showered together, hands gliding over each other's soap-slippery body, kissing and touching.

"Sure you can't skip your week in the woods?" he asked.

"Sure you can't take a later flight?"

They both laughed as they dried off. It was a frequent exchange when they got together. Darcy used the hairdryer, while Robert shaved, and when they finished, she picked up the trail of discarded clothes from the night before, tossing his on the bed and packing hers into her overnight bag.

He came up behind her, put his arms around her, and rested his chin on the top of her head. "You know, sweetness, sometime you're going to have to settle down. Can't keep traveling like this forever."

"But I can't imagine doing that in a city. Can you see yourself living anywhere else?"

"Not right now. That's where my clients are. Not much call for my experience in small towns, and I don't think the wildlife in the woods have any use for me at all." He turned her around to face him. "But I'm going to retire in a few years, and I'll go anywhere in the world to be with you then."

She bit her lip and held her breath before she looked up at him. "And in a few years, I'll give up my life as a nature photographer and meet you anywhere you want, even a small city."

He hugged her close. "Woman, you are the toughest negotiator I've ever known."

"But I bet none of them love you more than I do."

"I think you've got that right." With a laugh, he swatted her and gave her a quick kiss that turned into something deeper, something from the heart, sealing their promise.

Robert walked her to the Land Rover, and they kissed again, as the first light turned the sky pink and lavender.

Arms around each other, they watched the dawn, and he touched her cheek to turn her face toward his.

"Darcy, just to make this official, will you marry me?"

Back within mobile phone range after a week away, Darcy had found a page from a number she didn't recognize. She was dialing to check her voice mails first before calling, when the phone rang.

"Darcy?"

"Yes, this is Darcy."

"I'm Annette Miller. You're a friend of my brother Robert. I found your name on an email he was writing, and your number was in his phone."

Darcy sat down and closed her eyes. Her heart wanted to stop beating. "What happened?"

"I'm so sorry, Darcy, you don't even know me, and..."

"Where's Robert?"

Annette hesitated before answering. "He died six days ago. The hotel maid found him slumped over the computer." Annette kept talking, but the words didn't register. When Darcy could focus again, she learned Robert had already been buried. She mumbled something, not sure later what she'd said, and drove all night to the cottage. She'd kept the shutters closed and the lights off, living on packets of soup and the dehydrated foods in her emergency sack.

One night, she got up and took a shower, reliving their last moments together, crying under the pelting water long after it turned cold. She'd gone out to the beach facing the bay with her camera and caught the first glimmers of light.

The quiet woke Darcy. She opened the pantry door. Moonlight revealed the cottage was intact. She ran outside — the only evidence of the storm was broken tree limbs. She hurried back inside for her camera and down to the beach. Catching the first glow of morning over the bay, she whispered as she did every dawn, "Just a few more years before we're together."

A CONNECTION WITH GEORGE WASHINGTON

MARY MONTAGUE SIKES

D o you believe we are all connected in some way? Perhaps we are.

When I was a child, I spent long days chatting with my grandmother who was born in the late 1800s and knew people who fought in the Civil War. She knew people who knew people from the time of George Washington. My mother was also closely connected with people she admired from the nineteenth century. She adored anything historic, and at a time when research was difficult, Mother traced her ancestral roots back to the Revolutionary War so that she could join the Daughters of the American Revolution.

Because I grew up in Fredericksburg, Virginia, George Washington and homes related to his family played a big part in the early days of my life. My mother, who was fascinated with the city's history, belonged to the Kenmore Association and loved being one of the volunteers at this historic home. Kenmore, a Georgian-style brick mansion built in the 1700s before the Revolutionary War, was the home of George Washington's sister Betty Washington Lewis and her husband Fielding Lewis.

My mother always took me with her — an outing I enjoyed, but to this day, I cannot stand the thought of spicy gingerbread that was provided with the tea. I think of her beautifully attired in her stylish black hat and elegant black dress or suit, serving from the silver urn at Kenmore. As in colonial times, the popular gingerbread treat was prepared in a kitchen that was a separate building from the main house.

As a child, I was awestruck by the cannonball lodged in the thick brick wall of the historic mansion. Although I believed the cannonball came from the Revolution, it was actually embedded there during one of the Civil War battles waged in Fredericksburg.

When we lived in Fredericksburg, my mother became good friends with Mrs. Vivian Minor Fleming and her daughter Miss Annie Smith. In 1922, Mrs. Fleming led a fundraising campaign to buy Kenmore and was thus able to save it as an historic site. Her efforts led to the founding of the Kenmore Association, which in recent years has become the George Washington Foundation. Vice President Calvin Coolidge helped Mrs. Fleming and her associates to launch the campaign that saved Kenmore. "It must be preserved for patriotic America," Coolidge said.

As a token of friendship, Mrs. Fleming gave my mother a demitasse cup from the set used when she hosted a tea in honor of Calvin Coolidge. Mother treasured the gift, and I now have that china cup in my collection.

Being at Kenmore became quite a routine for me. I enjoyed wandering in the gardens and going to the nearby Mary Washington House, the home of the mother of George Washington. That house is another that was saved from destruction when plans were underway to disassemble the building and ship the parts to set up for display in the Chicago World's Fair of 1893.

When we lived in Fredericksburg, Kenmore and Mary Washington House were part of Virginia's Historic Garden Week. One year, my grandmother made beautiful colonial costumes for my mother, herself, and me to wear for the Garden Week events. I have studio photographs from that year, when as a five-year-old, I posed on the steps of Kenmore. For several weeks before, during, and after Garden Week, the local photographer who took my picture displayed an enlargement of it in his storefront window.

When I was old enough to go to school, I walked twelve long city blocks from our home located on a street by the University of Mary Washington to Lafayette Elementary School on the banks of the Rappahannock River. That school building served as a hospital during the Civil War and, to my dismay, still had blood-stained floors. The building now houses Central Rappahannock Regional Library.

Each day, to and from school, I hurried past Kenmore. During that time, an article came out in the newspaper about the ghost of Fielding Lewis. According to the story, the legendary builder of Kenmore could sometimes be seen riding his horse across the old plantation grounds. Fearing I might see this ghost, I would run as fast as I could along the block that bordered the grounds of the legendary old house.

At the time we lived in Fredericksburg, I knew little about Colonel Fielding Lewis except that he was the brother-in-law of George Washington. I later learned that during the Revolutionary War he loaned money to the state of Virginia to build and support a Fredericksburg gun factory. He was a patriot involved in outfitting ships, and although not a soldier, he earned the title "Colonel" as head of the militia for Spotsylvania County. He was never repaid the large debt owed him by the state, and he lost money during the war because he was unable to continue the mercantile business he had established with England. No longer a man of great wealth, Colonel Lewis died at Kenmore in December 1781, only a few weeks after the surrender of Cornwallis at Yorktown.

When we moved to West Point, my mother and I were both quite sad to leave Fredericksburg and its historic buildings. I thought we were leaving behind all our connections with George Washington. Not so.

As a young adult, I became the area correspondent for the Richmond News Leader and was asked to write an article about a grave marker in New Kent County placed on the possible gravesite of John Parke Custis, the only son of Martha Dandridge Custis Washington. Around 1960, a chapter of the Sons of the American Revolution placed the marker, according to Mrs. Frank Taylor who, along with her husband, owned the property at that time.

The day I visited a small grove of trees on a farm along the Pamunkey River I found the tombstone bearing the name of John Parke Custis. I learned about the close connection between George Washington and the huge Eltham plantation that once encompassed 6,000 acres in New Kent County. I found out that prior to the Revolutionary War, when Washington was a member of the House of Burgesses in Williamsburg, he spent much of his time on the plantation.

John Parke Custis died at Eltham Plantation the night of October 19, 1781, the day Cornwallis surrendered at Yorktown. Custis, stepson of George Washington, served as an *aide-de-camp* to the General during the siege at Yorktown. Washington is believed to have ridden on horseback through the night back to Eltham, arriving just as the twenty-seven year old man died of camp fever (probably yellow fever).

After the death of John Parke Custis, George Washington adopted his two youngest children, Eleanor (Nelly) Parke Custis and George Washington Parke Custis. I was especially intrigued to learn that the only daughter of George Washington Custis became the wife of General Robert E. Lee. Strange how history binds us together. Marriage connected George Washington and General Robert E. Lee, two of our country's most memorable men, both dedicated to their causes.

When she was a child, my mother listened to discussions by family members about people from earlier generations. She heard about the connection of our ancestor, Joseph Gravely, with the Revolution and with General Washington as he witnessed the surrender of Cornwallis at Yorktown. Her early contacts created a lifelong love of history for my mother who later researched these connections when she wanted to join the DAR.

I remember the lovely days at historic Kenmore. I can still see my mother smiling in front of the big silver service, holding a china cup and pouring tea. I never saw Fielding Lewis riding across the grounds, and I am glad.

THANK YOU, FIELDING LEWIS

MARY MONTAGUE SIKES

Thank you, Fielding Lewis, for all you gave
land of our free, home of our brave.
Patriot on a plantation,
In failing health you found a way
to aid the cause, strong and true
to follow great generals of your time.

Independence, revolution
Fielding Lewis, you were the man for those days.
Bullets, guns, you gave your all.
What cost freedom for the American way?

Did you see the Yorktown surrender?
Or were you bound to old Fredericksburg
where what you did helped win the war?
Your own funds diminished
Never repaid for your trouble to end the fight,
your life was changed. Did you look back?

Sometimes today in old Kenmore
you are seen seated at your dark desk
Rifling through papers
frowning, hoping to recover your wealth.
Did you have regrets you gave your all
for freedom and the American way?

Sometimes, you still ride your horse
across diminished grounds of old Kenmore.
Do you still ride there?

I would be frightened by the sight
of a ghostly man in revolutionary uniform
riding there today.

Still, I look for you and wonder how you felt
Patriot on a plantation that you could fund no more.
A lonely man lost in his despair
Thank you, Fielding Lewis, good colonel,
for all you gave
Land of our free, home of our brave.

LOVE THY NEIGHBOR

JULIE LEVERENZ

Thehe day after Fred and I came back from visiting the grandchildren, Amanda's name appeared in the *Virginia Gazette's* Police Blotter. That same afternoon, I was waiting for the light at Olde Towne and Longhill Roads, about a mile from home, when she trudged down from the bus stop and crossed in front of me. It was a drizzly afternoon in early November, one of those days that can't make up its mind whether to rain or snow. Longhill Road was scary enough in a car, never mind on foot, so when the light changed I pulled off the road ahead of her and waited.

Watching her approach in the rearview mirror, I had second thoughts. The Amanda who lived down at the end of our cul-de-sac with her little girl—Corinne—was shy but friendly, with a sweet smile. This woman, hunched into a ragged parka with a tan-drab watch cap pulled low over her eyes, plodded toward me with defeat ringing from each step. She came alongside and I lowered the window. *Even if it's not Amanda, I could offer her a ride.*

"Amanda?" I called.

She hesitated, glanced in, and looked away. Nestled in the cavernous hood of her parka her pale face looked small, pinched, and wary.

"Amanda?" I repeated. "Amanda Carpenter?" She straightened slightly. "I live up the street from you. Cindy Hanscome. We've talked at neighborhood picnics." She nodded a wordless greeting. "Would you like a ride?"

Amanda shrank into herself. "That's okay," she said, "I can walk." Her voice was soft, almost a whisper.

"But it's raining," I persisted. "It's cold. Come on, get in."

She climbed in, pressed herself against the passenger door, and fixed her eyes on the floor. She smelled of stale cigarettes and unwashed hair.

Dying to know the details behind the Police Blotter, I prodded her with gentle questions while I drove into Kings Grant. Her answers were vague, jumbled. Traffic ticket... insurance... took driver's license... electric bill... no heat, lights... Child Services... jail...

I shuddered. "Is Corinne okay?"

Amanda mumbled, "They took her away."

"Oh, Amanda," I said. "I'm so sorry."

She was silent.

When I saw the tall weeds in Amanda's yard I realized I hadn't been down to that end of the street since our little dog Buster died four months ago. Amanda got out and pushed through the scraggly, overgrown shrubbery crowding the path to her front stoop. At the door, she turned and gave me a shy, half-wave.

That night, while I sorted the laundry from our trip, I said to Fred, "I feel like I need to do something. When I rolled out the trash just now I looked down the street and her house is like a black hole."

He peered at me over his reading glasses. "Are you sure you're not just being nosy?"

"Well, maybe a little," I conceded. "But I hate to think of her all by herself in the cold and dark. Maybe tomorrow I'll take her that loaf of banana bread in the freezer."

Fred's eyes flashed concern. "You don't know anything about her. Don't forget she was arrested."

"Child neglect isn't murder," I retorted.

The next day I knocked on her door, banana bread in hand. Amanda let me in, mumbled an apology, and led me through cluttered rooms painted in ominous dark browns, purples, and greens, with ragged roller-brush strokes stopping a foot below the ceiling. I recoiled, understanding instantly why they took little Corinne. In the kitchen, cigarette butts and crusted dishes clogged the sink; flies swarmed around the refrigerator. I almost gagged on the stench of rotting food and cigarettes. Months of unopened mail littered the kitchen table.

With Amanda trailing meekly behind, I went into the living room and pulled back the heavy window drapes. Sunshine struggled through the smoke-dusky windows. Amanda blinked.

I could not leave her like that. Over the next few days, I took her to the Salvation Army to get her electricity on and helped her wade through the mail. I drove her to the Industrial Park and coached her on what to say—the foreman took pity and gave her job back. I took her to her court-ordered psychiatric evaluation. I saw with relief that the contract she had already signed to sell her house to a scavenger wasn't a bad deal, leaving her with enough money to live on if she kept her job, found a cheap apartment, and managed her spending. I took her to Consumer Credit Counseling.

Within a few weeks I was able to piece together her backstory. An afterthought child whose mother died when she was thirteen, Amanda lived in a clapboard shack on an Appalachian hillside with her father. Corinne, born on Amanda's thirty-first birthday, was the product of an abusive uncle; Amanda's vengeful older brother murdered the uncle and died in a prison fight. After her father's death, Amanda sold the farm, took the money and seven-year-old Corinne and fled to her dream of a fairy-tale life in Williamsburg. But after a year and a half, the dream became a nightmare: when the money ran out, her life started toppling like a trail of dominoes.

She wouldn't talk about Corinne. Every time I asked, she gave a sad little shrug and said only, "They took her away."

Early in January, Amanda received a subpoena to appear for her adjudication hearing. Terrified, she asked me to go with her. In the imposing courtroom, we sat on hard pew-like benches until the bailiff called her name. Standing before the judge, dwarfed by the court-appointed attorney beside her, Amanda looked like a shivering puppy expecting to be kicked.

"Ms. Carpenter." The judge looked sternly at Amanda. "You have been charged with felony child abuse." Reading from the paper before him, he continued, "On the night of October 24, you left your nine-year-old daughter alone in a house with no heat and no lights when you went to the store. As a result of your neglect, your daughter tripped, hit her head, and subsequently died of her injuries."

I gasped aloud. The judge shot me a warning glance. "Ms. Carpenter," he said, "do you wish to change the guilty plea that you made at the pretrial hearing?"

The lawyer leaned down and spoke to Amanda. "No, Your Honor," she squeaked.

The judge studied the papers. My mind reeled with shock and dread; I was sure Amanda would go to prison. But when he looked up, the judge's eyes were surprisingly kind.

"I have reviewed the circumstances and the psychiatrist's evaluation. In the absence of willful intent, I do not believe that incarceration will be beneficial. Therefore, I sentence you to one year, suspended, with mandatory counseling, to be reviewed in twelve months' time." He smacked down the gavel, hard wood on hard wood. "Keep in mind," he said, "if you fail to meet the terms of your probation, you will go to jail."

Still grappling with my emotions, I guided Amanda out of the courtroom. Her head was bowed; when she spoke I had to lean down to hear.

"I had to go get some medicine for her cough," she murmured.

Tears welled in my eyes. If only I'd gotten involved sooner, rallied the neighbors. Even though Fred and I were away, somebody could have sat with Corinne. I put my arm around Amanda's shoulders. She felt like a limp rag doll.

Ever so slowly, with the help of her counselor, the doctors at the Olde Towne Clinic, her probation officer, and me, Amanda started to peek out of her paralyzing depression. She joined the women's Bible study class at my church. One afternoon I went looking for Fred and found him mowing her grass.

I felt I was part of a team—my role was to reinforce and help her carry out the guidance she got from the professionals. Just like that day when I first opened her living room curtains, I wanted to bring light into her troubled life. We settled into a routine: I went over every Tuesday or Wednesday, depending on her shift schedule, and we went through the mail and talked about her action plan for the week. With all of us to help her, she found a cheap apartment in a decent neighborhood. She quit smoking. She brightened, made eye contact, and smiled more. Gradually, she became able to talk about Corinne without crying.

At the end of the year, when the judge released her from probation and reduced her charge from felony child abuse to misdemeanor, Amanda and I rejoiced. Afterwards, in the courthouse parking lot, I asked her what she'd learned. She thought a moment, then said, "It's like I've got the pattern all cut out. Now I just need to stitch it together."

I looked at her in astonishment, thinking, *Wow*.

At that moment, I believed she could do it. Her face shone, as if she were reflecting back at me all the light she had absorbed over the year. I was proud of her and proud to have been part of her team.

But it turned out that the planning and execution required to do the stitching was beyond her. One by one, her dominoes started tipping again, then falling. The factory laid her off, saying she worked too slowly. Colonial Williamsburg's housekeeping said the same, but kept her on until she failed to call in when she stayed home sick for three days. She stopped coming to church. She started smoking again.

Without the court-ordered professionals, I struggled to fill the roles of counselor and probation officer. But where they had the threat of jail, I was powerless. One evening I moaned to Fred, "Amanda isn't stupid. She knows, but she doesn't *do*. She does whatever appeals to her right now. This morning she showed me an expensive purse she bought because she thought it was pretty. She won't carry anything but that old backpack, for pity's sake, so I talked her into returning it. Last week she signed up for ten magazine subscriptions to get a chance at a million-dollar lottery. It's gotten so I dread going over there, wondering if I can reverse whatever bad choices she's made." Pushing back from the dinner table, I threw up my hands and wailed, "It's so frustrating. She's forty-two years old. I can't monitor her every minute!"

Fred leaned toward me. "She did manage without you for forty-two years. Maybe it's time for you to back off."

"She didn't manage, her father did. Since then she's only managed to run through the money." I shook my head. "Sometimes I feel like I'm all that's keeping her from living under a bridge."

Unseeing, I contemplated the remains of our dinner. Finally I said, "I don't know if I'm hanging on for her or for me. Maybe I want to believe that I can fix her."

Fred sat back, chuckling. "You know you can't fix her. 'Fess up: deep down, you like fixing her messes."

I threw my wadded-up napkin at him.

But I had to admit that Fred was right. A part of me enjoyed swooping into her tragic soap-opera life each week with solutions and advice, like Cinderella's fairy godmother.

Unlike a fairy godmother, however, I had no magic wand. To my dismay, Amanda continued to slide. I ramped up my efforts—our Tuesday visits became Tuesday, Thursday, and then Saturday visits. When I wasn't with her,

I worried about her. Before long, my short drives over to her apartment became mental tugs of war between resentment and responsibility: *Amanda's not going to change, so why am I wasting my time?* versus *You got yourself into this; you're all she has.*

One dreary fall morning I came out of the bedroom to a dark house. Irritated, I yanked back the front curtains. *First one up, opens up*—and this was the second time in a week that Fred hadn't bothered. Stomping into the kitchen, I yelled to the empty house, "Do I have to do everything for everybody?"

I slumped in a chair with my coffee, stoking my annoyance with several more of Fred's recent transgressions. *Can't he see I've got my hands full with Amanda?*

A gust of wind bounced an acorn against the window sill, making me look up. For a few moments I watched wet leaves swirl and settle onto the sodden, tired back yard. I felt like one of those wretched leaves, spiraling down to a thankless end. A tear trickled down my cheek. As I brushed it away, Fred's words came back to me: "Maybe it's time for you to back off." And suddenly I understood.

It's not Fred.

Amanda had dragged me down too far. But in truth, I knew it wasn't Amanda, either. If Amanda wasn't going to change, then I had to. As I drained my coffee, I resolved to put together a plan, steel myself, and do it.

I never got the chance. Two days later, I found Amanda's apartment door ajar and her backpack sprawled on the kitchen counter. The hospital found my number in her pocket and called me: Amanda was in the ER with a pulmonary embolism. I rushed out to Sentara Medical

Center.

She lay, small and pale, on a white-sheeted bed heaped with thin, nubby blankets. An oxygen compressor hissed, IV fluids dripped, and monitors beeped, while the muffled hubbub of doctors, nurses, and equipment shuttled back and forth outside the room. I took her hand, and she clung to me like a baby grasps her mother's finger. Her eyes glistened with fear.

"This is what killed my mother," she whispered. Her breathing was labored.

"Well it's not going to kill you," I said firmly, hoping it was true. At that moment, my need to see her through this crisis eclipsed everything else, including my back-off plan. *One more fix.*

She tugged at my hand and I leaned closer. "I'm sorry I'm such a bother," she said.

"Don't be. I'm just glad they called."

She rolled her head side to side, struggling for air. "You're awfully nice to me. Thank you for being my friend." Her thin chest heaved with the effort.

"Shh," I said. "Rest. I'll be here."

This is why I keep showing up, I thought. *Amanda needs me, and when I'm with her, I feel like a good person.*

Closing her eyes, Amanda relaxed her grip on my hand. I gazed down at her with wonder. *Maybe being her friend is good enough.*

Three days later, despite the doctors' best efforts, Amanda died. She had gotten one of the nurses to help her make a rudimentary will, leaving her few meager belongings to me. Most of her things went to Goodwill or the dump, but I saved the photos—Corinne's school pictures and an old album. As I leafed through the water-stained album's brittle pages, looking at black and white pictures of people whose stories I would never know, Fred came over and stood by my shoulder. After a moment he wrapped his arms around me and rested his chin on my trembling head.

LESSONS FROM GRANDFATHER JIM

ANN SKELTON

G randfather Jim had a secret. He was able to do something that no one else in the town of Hooper's Creek could do. He could talk to the animals. Each morning he listened to the birds sing and watched the sun rise slowly over the great James River just beyond his creek. Most mornings a brilliant green and brown wood duck came out of the tall grasses along the edge of the water and sat quietly nearby. A woodpecker nodded his red head from a perch in the willow tree.

When Jim was a young sea captain and his hair was still black he sailed his ferryboat back and forth across the James River, carrying cars and people and seed for the farms on the other side. The owner of the ferryboat gave Grandfather a hat with gold braid and two stars to show the people that he was the commander of the ferry. Grandfather stood very tall when he wore his hat. Each evening he polished the stars and placed the hat on a high shelf where only he could reach it. Each morning he proudly placed his captain's hat on his head at a jaunty angle.

Grandfather Jim lived in a tiny house nestled among the pines and birches of Hooper's Creek. Sometimes neighbors brought Jim plates of cookies or jars of pickles. They worried about the old man living by himself, but he was never lonely. After all, the birds and wildlife around Hooper's Creek kept him company.

Grandfather had visitors from time to time. He was

especially happy when his grandchildren Joey and Ethan and their pesky little sister Maggie came to stay. They climbed trees in the afternoons and chased fireflies in the evenings while Grandfather watched over them, sipping his mug of coffee. When Grandfather whispered to the sparrows, the tiny birds cocked their heads and whistled in reply. The children begged Grandfather to teach them his special language so they too could speak to the ducks and waterfowl that lived around the inlet.

The key was to listen carefully when the birds and the animals called to each other and speak to them with a very soft voice. The animals liked his gentle face and soft voice. That's why they taught Grandfather their language.

Grandfather loved his rambunctious little grandchildren and taught them many things about the creeks and winding inlets that carved into the land along the James River. The one thing he could not teach them was how to talk to the birds and animals.

"The birds and the ducks have to teach you their words themselves," Grandfather said. "You have to listen."

But the children were impatient. They tried to listen quietly to the wood duck that sailed around the inlet, but someone would always start to giggle and away flew the duck. The children were just plain noisy.

Until they met Miss Lily and her friend, Captain Charles Canada Goose.

Miss Lily, a snow-white swan, established her home in plain view of Grandfather's cottage on Hooper's Creek. Grandfather was particularly fond of the beautiful swan from the moment he saw her swimming gracefully in the inlet. As the children watched, they saw that Miss Lily had a broken wing that dragged on the ground when she walked. Grandfather knew that Miss Lily was angry that her wing was broken, and that made her cranky. She squawked and flew at her friends for no reason. She didn't want other birds or animals to know she couldn't fly, so she flapped her wings to pretend she was flying whenever a rabbit or a duck looked her way.

"Grandfather, how did Miss Lily hurt her wing?" Joey asked.

"Well Joey, it's a sad story. I was standing by the mailbox the day it happened. Miss Lily began to rise into the sky over the rough country road. You know that to take off swans need a long runway, almost like an airplane. That day she was flapping her wings and slowly rising into the sky, but she could not find the warm air current to carry her high above the houses and cars. She was a few feet in the air when the truck came around the bend to deliver the mail. It hit her wing and sent her falling to the ground."

"Poor Lily, that must have hurt her," Maggie said.

"Well, her wing is healed now," Grandfather said, "but she's still lonely and still cranky."

"Look Maggie," Ethan said, "her neck is in the shape of an S, and her white feathers shine in the sun."

"Cool," Maggie said.

Early one March morning a mighty flock of Canada geese appeared in the sky over the great river and headed for Hooper's Creek. They looked wonderful flying high in the sky with their long necks stretched forward. They flew into the inlet in perfect formation, landed in the water, splashed Miss Lily, and squawked in their loudest voices to announce their arrival. They may have looked graceful, but they were very rude geese.

They teased Miss Lily by climbing into her nest. Worst of all, they tried to steal her food. They climbed up the steep bank beside the creek and nibbled the bits of corn that Grandfather put there for her. They didn't even ask.

Miss Lily tried to guard her home and her food. Though she couldn't fly, she was a graceful swimmer. She patrolled the edge of the bank and chased away the bad-mannered Canada geese day after day. Unfortunately, these geese were not only mean, but very smart. Each day they sent one goose ahead that raced to Miss Lily's food. She ruffled her wings and chased that goose down to the other end of the creek. While she was chasing, the other geese swam very fast, climbed on shore, and began to eat Lily's corn. Miss Lily became more tired and angry, but she never gave up.

Each day she fluffed her feathers to make herself look enormous and lunged at the geese stealing her corn. That frightened the geese and made them fly away over the water. Still, every day those unwanted guests returned to tease her.

Grandfather and the children waited patiently each day to watch the scene. They felt sorry for Miss Lily because she had to fight off so many enemies.

"They are good flyers, those Canada geese," said Grandfather as he watched them flying in formation and squawking noisily. "I don't know if Miss Lily will be able to keep them away."

Miss Lily clearly needed help.

One day after watching the geese come in for a landing, Grandfather noticed that one goose stood out from all the rest. This goose was special. He was the biggest and the tallest goose, with an extra-long, shiny black neck. Grandfather recognized him as an officer immediately, and named him Captain Charles C. Goose of the Royal Canadian Flying Geese.

"Look, he's helping Miss Lily chase away the others," Joey said.

Time after time when one of the rude Canada geese neared Miss Lily's bank, Captain Charles C. Goose pursued him until the robber goose flew away. Joey also noticed a very small goose that was hiding among the tall grasses along the edge of Hooper's Creek.

"Look at that small black and grey goose," Joey said. "I think Captain Charles is watching out for her."

"Maybe she is his special friend," Grandfather said.

"I'll call her Sarah-Goose," Maggie said. "Look what a good swimmer she is."

Sarah-Goose was an acrobat. She turned somersaults in the water and dove deep so that only her white tail feathers showed. Captain Charles C. Goose tried to do tricks too, but he was too big.

"Silly goose," Maggie said, using a phrase she heard her mother say.

Sarah-Goose was afraid of the noisy geese who had invaded Hooper's Creek. She stayed close to Captain Charles when he wasn't helping Miss Lily. One day Grandfather noticed that the rude geese stopped coming to the pond. At last Captain Charles had chased that rude gang away. After that Captain Charles C. Goose and Sarah swam quietly and stayed together all the time.

"Look, Grandfather," Joey said. "Miss Lily is swimming with Sarah-Goose and Captain. They must like each other."

"I think Miss Lily was lonely all by herself," Maggie said. "Now she has Captain Charles and Sarah-Goose to keep her company."

A few days later the children were on the porch drawing. Ethan was shading in a grey bunny while Joey bent over his drawing pad and chewed his pencil.

"You know, I haven't noticed Sarah-Goose swimming in the creek today."

The children peered over the porch railing searching Grandfather's front yard. Then they walked along the edge of the inlet to see if she was in the middle of the tall grasses. Sarah-Goose was nowhere to be found.

"Grandfather, we've looked everywhere. Where could she be?" Maggie started to cry.

Grandfather stepped outside to inquire of Captain Charles where Sarah-Goose might be. The children watched from the porch as Grandfather nodded and stepped away from the Captain.

"Come inside children and I'll explain." Grandfather pushed his captain's hat back on his head and scratched his chin. "Well, it seems that our friend Sarah has hidden a nest of eggs and only Captain Charles knows where it is," Grandfather explained. "The Captain wants to make sure that you children won't look for the nest."

"We won't. We promise. Cross my heart." Joey and Ethan and Maggie were all talking at the same time. "When can we see the little geese?" Maggie asked.

"They're called goslings, silly," Ethan said.

Grandfather and the children watched quietly every morning to see if Sarah would return.

"Sarah is very careful. She doesn't want other animals or even geese to know where she is hiding. She wants to keep the eggs safe," Grandfather explained.

Joey grew impatient waiting for Sarah to return. He suspected that Sarah-Goose went to a quiet place in the marshy area across the creek. He too loved the quiet of the water and thought it would be a good place for a secret nest. One chilly morning, he decided to explore the high grasses around the inlet.

"C'mon, Ethan. Wake up," Joey called as he shook Ethan's shoulder. "Put on this life jacket. We're going exploring." The boys tiptoed outside and pushed Grandfather's old rowboat out into the water. They knew to stay away from the strong waters of the James River. Joey began to row through the early morning mist toward the end of Hooper's Creek. The rising sun cast a pink glow through the layer of fog. Everything was silent on the inlet. The two boys whispered to each other, careful not to break the spell of the morning. Joey dipped his oars into the creek. Suddenly, a frog croaked and both boys jumped.

"It feels creepy, Joey. Maybe we should go back," Ethan whispered.

Joey shook his head. "Just a little bit more, Ethan. We're almost there."

Joey kept rowing when a sudden loud squawking broke

into the quiet morning. Ethan ducked into the bottom of the boat. Joey jumped and almost lost the oars. Charles C. Goose was flapping his wings at the rowboat and diving at Joey like a fighter pilot.

Joey covered his head with his arms. He took hold of the oars and began rowing as fast as he could back to Grandfather's cottage.

Grandfather was waiting for the two brothers on the lawn when, shivering, they tied up the rowboat. "You youngsters know you're not allowed on the water without a grown-up. I was worried sick waiting for you."

Joey and Ethan were sad all morning. It was the first time Grandfather had ever scolded them, and they worried about the incident with Captain Charles. Was he turning mean?

Joey was staring at the floor when he felt Grandfather's hand patting his shoulder.

"Why did Captain Charles do that to me, Grandfather? I wouldn't hurt him or Sarah. Doesn't he know that?" Joey went on staring at the floor remembering Charles C. Goose squawking and flying at them.

"Can I tell you a secret, Grandfather?" Joey said. "I think I understood what Captain Charles C. Goose said to me this morning when he scared me. He said, 'Danger, danger, get out!' He thought I was the enemy."

"Well, I'll be! You really were listening. I guess at that moment you seemed like a danger to Sarah."

The next week Grandfather and the children learned why Joey was dangerous to the Captain. Joey was the first to see Ms. Sarah-Goose walking proudly onto the lawn at Grandfather's cottage in the early morning. She was leading six fuzzy yellow goslings. They were wobbling but trying hard to keep up with Sarah.

"Now we can watch Sarah teach her goslings to turn somersaults in the water," Maggie said. "They look so soft."

"Hear that squawking Maggie? Sarah-Goose said to stay far away," Joey replied softly.

Grandfather smiled at Joey, leaned over and placed his gold braided Captain's hat squarely on Joey's head.

DEVIL IN THE DETAILS

PAMELA K. KINNEY

T hey say the devil is in the details. Most especially when one sold their soul to the Devil, in a literal sense. Then life and death becomes extremely important.

I should have read that contract better before I signed it in blood ten years ago.

Jenna tossed back the glass of scotch she held. The amber liquid burned a path down her throat to her stomach. The glass clinked as she set it down next to the empty bottle. It toppled over and spilled the scotch across the table's surface.

A giggle escaped her. Who gave a damn about a mess on one measly table? Or that she had never been so drunk in her life. Not with her soul in trouble. Hell put things into perspective.

Fine, she got her deal; millionaire status and her family's plantation house still in her name. Being rich enabled her to make her home once again into a true Southern lady in all her glory. It meant Jenna's family name of London was once again an honored one in Gloucester and her home the way it had been in 1760.

Jenna stumbled into an overstuffed chair and drifted off to sleep. Sleep that brought on the same dream she'd been having for the past year. Or was it a memory?

She had visited Rosewell Plantation ten years ago. In 1725 it was home to the Page family. The fire in 1916 brought most of the structure down, leaving it nothing but bare bones of former Southern opulence. Besides a ghost story attached to it, a legend claimed the first owner Mann Page died in the front hall before the completion of the place, due to "God striking him down for his excess."

She didn't understand why she visited that day. Her business was about to go down the shitter and her house was for sale on the auction block to save her from ending up on the street. The damned economy had not only ruined many in America, it brought her along for the ride.

It was a lovely spring Saturday morning when she visited the place. She breathed in the crisp, fresh chill of the air, full of flowers blooming and tree buds renewing. There were still enough of the remnants of winter that she wished she had thought to grab a sweater before leaving home.

"Here, Jenna London. Catch!"

Jenna whipped around and a light jacket fell into her arms. A good-looking man with longish black hair and black eyes sat on the front steps of Rosewell with an amused look on his face. He hadn't been there a minute ago. Except for the chirping birds, Jenna felt no one other than her was visiting the historical ruins.

The man rose in one fluid movement to his feet and sauntered over to her.

God, his eyes have no pupils!

"Yes, that is right. I am not human. Not mortal either."

Heart pounding, she threw the jacket to the ground and wiped her hands on her jeans. "Just what, or who, are you?"

"I've been known by many names over the centuries... Lucifer, Satan, the Great Horned God, Mammon, Dragon, Father of Lies, Abaddon, Accuser, Apollyon, Beast,

Beelzebub, Belial... look, let's get on to why I am here and not waste time with who I am."

"I don't think the Devil just decided to take a tour of a historical house of Gloucester."

"No, but it's a perfect place to strike a deal. After all, it's where I got the soul of the original owner of this place. He made a deal with me too."

"Why me?"

"Look, Jenna. May I call you Jenna, and not Miss London? You are on the last dregs of desperation, about to lose what's left of an old family plantation that your ancestor built. I want to help." Several what appeared to be legal papers appeared in his left hand.

"Why?"

"I could say I am a stand-up kind of guy. But honestly, I want your soul. You're no innocent, haven't been for a long time, but still, your soul would be a great addition for my collection in Hell."

So brutally honest for the Father of Lies. He was right. She didn't want to lose her house. Wanted to keep her business and strike it rich. Here, in Virginia! Not in the nowhere land of Alaska, living in her sister's house in Fairbanks. A sister she'd never gotten along with and who would be sure to point out every chance she got that Jenna was a failure and lost a house that been in the family forever. Alice had always been a bitch and jealous that Jenna was the oldest and inherited London Hall.

She let out a breath. "Where do I sign?"

The Devil smiled and scratched the index finger of her right hand with a sharp claw. Blood welled up. "Right here, on the dotted line with your blood."

Jenna awoke. Her neck had a crick in it and the rage of an alcohol-laced headache was tearing her head apart. With her mouth dry and her body shaking, she forced herself out of the chair. She knew how her death would be when Lucifer came to collect his newest possession. That part of the contract she remembered well.

She'd be double-damned if she gave him her death the way he wanted. Maybe it was time she found church again. Grabbing her car keys hanging by the front hall and rushing out the door, she got in her car and drove away, dust rising in a fog behind her. She hadn't been to Abingdon Episcopal Church in ten years, not since she'd lost her faith and began the downspin to Hell's grasping fingers, but she knew the way, sober or drunk. She'd beat the Devil at his own game.

No moon or stars lit her way. Ominous dark clouds rode the night sky. Thank God, for her....The brilliant beams from her car lights dimmed, then died.

Her breathing had a hitch in it. *Bump. Bump. Bump.* God, that's her heart! She brought up the speed, even though she couldn't see the road well. If she was lucky, people were safe and sound in their beds, not sharing the road with her at this time of night.

Oh, thank God, there's Abingdon! The church shone in the darkness, a beacon as it'd been for 350 years.

Suddenly, her car swerved to the left. She fought the steering wheel, but couldn't get control of the vehicle back. The street she had been on vanished, replaced by the shadowy skeleton of Rosewell. Helpless, she gave up the fight as her car soared toward the place and then through it. She'd been right; Rosewell was a ghost of itself. The next moment she felt agony as her car slammed into a large tree.

A piece of the windshield cracked free and cut into her forehead, silencing all thought and life in Jenna.

The Devil watched as the new dawn painted the sky in a splatter of pastel colors. With a snap of his fingers, what remained of the car and Jenna vanished and the tree went back to normal. It wouldn't do for any mortal to wonder what had happened to the tree.

Jenna thought she could beat him. Make his contract null by interference of the heavenly sort. No one had ever outsmarted him. Not any true blue mortal, anyway. It was all in the miniscule fine print she missed, right beneath the part about how she might die when her time came. That print nullified everything with the words, "Unless Lucifer changes the details of the where and how of the death." Just like Mann Page's signed contract specified that Rosewell would go on forever with Page's death. But the fine print for that contract said, "… forever… unless Lucifer decides differently."

Lucifer snorted. He could do whatever he damned well please.

He was the Father of Lies, after all.

META

CARL J. SHIRLEY

"Can we turn these off now?" Dari asked. "I can't see my feet and the air ionization is getting itchy." Noll turned at the sound of Dari's voice, unable to see anything other than an errant refraction of light. This was due to the cloaking field that kept Dari invisible under the midday sun. There was a clear trail of flattened grass through the sea of brown, meter-tall switchgrass, a sign of their passage that even the cloaks could not hide. It was better than being in the open, though, exposed to Sentinel surveillance.

"It's about half a kilometer to the tree line," Noll replied. "We'll turn off the cloaks when we reach cover." He pressed forward through the tall grass.

"I thought we were going to a bay?" Dari asked. "This looks nothing like a bay."

"Susquehanna river valley. Thousands of years ago it was the Chesapeake Bay. Once the Neo-Laurentide Ice Sheet melts, it'll be one again. This climate provides the perfect conditions for our recovery operation."

"Walking seven kilometers through snake infested grass seems less than perfect to me."

"The snakes can no more see you than the Sentinels. But all this pointless chatter might attract some attention. And the cottonmouths are not the worst local predator that the Cherubim restored." Noll scanned the surrounding grass with renewed vigilance, prompted by his own exaggerations to take greater care. The retinal displays implanted in his eyes identified only grass, insects, and snakes in the immediate vicinity. Ahead, the tree line lit up with information on southern red oak, black gum, and hickory trees.

"Great," Dari whispered. Noll had wished to bring someone more useful along on this expedition, but the Meta had insisted that Dari was his only option. No one else could replace her or join them. One didn't argue with a Meta, and certainly not one of the guardian machines old enough to trace its circuitry and programming back to the exodus. The Meta had been right about the orbital insertion points and the clear landing path down to the river valley. Almost too easy a task, if you didn't count the seven-kilometer hike. And even that was pleasant enough this far south of the ice sheet.

As they reached the tree line, Noll suppressed his wonder at so many tall trees clustered so close together. His job right now was to scan the forest for any surveillance equipment. No doubt the Sentinels and their Cherubim masters were more than capable of hiding surveillance monitors from the likes of him, but after thoroughly scanning the surrounding forest, he decided it was safe enough to turn off the cloaks.

"What the frack is up with the trees on this planet?" Dari asked as the cloak dissolved around her. "So many and so tall." The shifting camouflage pattern on her thermal flight suit hid her almost as well under the dappled sunlight of the forest as the cloak had, with only her pale face and tight braid of auburn hair conspicuous.

"They evolved here. It's where they belong." Noll's own face was considerably darker, etched with the bright metallic lines of his sensor net. The pattern was a swirl of silver and gold that fed data to the retinal implants in his eyes.

"So did humans," Dari observed, looking up into the canopy, still enchanted with the trees.

"Yeah," Noll agreed. "Let's go." He moved deeper into the forest, the retinal map displaying data surreptitiously gathered from the Sentinels own satellite system to guide him to the coordinates.

"You think anyone else has been back here?" Dari asked. "Since the banishment?"

"Some have tried. Others have claimed to. Most never made it out."

"Would the Sentinels kill or capture?"

"Can't say. What use would they have for humans?"

"They are restorers, right? Humans were as much a natural part of this planet as the trees and the snakes."

"That's true," Noll said. "But most humans from the last few millennia are too wired up with wetware and other bio-integrated technologies to make good candidates for natural restoration." The trail forward angled up, the forest canopy thinning slightly as they reached the top of a small rise. "Here." He stopped. "This is where we need to dig." He unzipped a pocket on his jumpsuit, pulled out a small gray capsule and dropped it. It split open as it hit the ground, small silver grains spilling out onto the dark soil.

"Will those nanobots attract any attention?" Dari stepped back as the grains swirled across the ground, an undulating puddle of silver sand growing as it dug into the earth, devouring a meter-wide circle of soil.

"Maybe," Noll said. "But not as much as a conversion beam, and I didn't bring a shovel."

"A what?"

"Very old tech," he explained. "A manual digging tool."
The mass of silver sand was bubbling now as the bots
finished their work. The ground soil, having been converted
into the nanobot grains, was now streaming out of the hole
and down the hill where it collected into a lifeless mass
before converting back into soil. As the last of it trickled
down the hill, Noll looked into the hole. The nanobots
had dug a perfect circle into the ground, stopping when
they uncovered an object composed of the preprogramed
materials. "There it is," he said. Dari joined him and looked
into the meter and a half deep hole. A large, dark object
was at the bottom. It looked heavy.

"Did you bring any antigravity hoisters?" she asked.

"No," he said as he hopped down into the hole. "Some
things we'll just have to do the old-fashioned way." He
examined the object, trying to decide if even his enhanced
human musculature could lift it. It was a half-meter across,
dark-grey metallic cube, smooth on all the sides he could
see and obviously having suffered very little wear for the
20,000 years it spent under bay and forest. He nudged the
cube and decided it was too heavy to lift. But then he wasn't
interested in the object as much as the treasure within.
Bracing himself against the inside of the hole provided
enough leverage for him to move the cube around, and
soon he discovered an access door. Fortunately for Noll
the Meta had provided him with a compatible energy cell
that could be plugged into a port on the front of the door
to power the inactive touchpad. He fished the palm-sized
cylinder from his pocket and plugged it in, watching as the
touchpad rebooted. The Meta had said that after so many

centuries the access code for the door would reset to four zeroes, which he entered. At that the safe door popped open.

"Don't need to lift the safe," Noll explained as he reached inside, "just need to lift the treasure." He pulled a book out of the safe. A flimsy paperback with a blood red cover that looked rather creased and worn. "Salinger," he said, passing the book up to Dari.

"Holy crap," she whispered as she opened the pages. "It's a complete copy."

"Twain," Noll passed up another book. "Poe. Faulkner. Fitzgerald. Styron. Shakespeare. Vonnegut. Bester." Dari unzipped a pocket on her jumpsuit and pulled out a silver artifact bag for each book that Noll passed up to her. The last book, Noll held onto as he climbed out of the hole.

"How did all of these get down there?" Dari asked.

"The prized literary collection of an early 22nd century citizen of what was then Virginia. He lived on a boat following the sea level rise of that era. Kept his most valuable books in a specially designed safe, one created to protect them from both time and the elements. Worked very well for such old tech."

"How'd they end up at the bottom of the bay?"

"Boat was lost in a storm," he responded as he started to thumb through the last book. He'd never entirely believed what the Meta had told him about this book, about the need to close the paradox it had created. He'd been motivated enough by the thought of recovering the lost literature to undertake this mission. But now that he was here, book in hand, he had to scan the pages as fast as quantum processors that enhanced his human brain would allow. He could only read 1,410 words into the story before the paradox forced him to close the book.

"Which book is that?" Dari asked.

"The one we came for," Noll showed her the cover. *Harboring Secrets: Tales & Reflections from the Chesapeake Bay Writers.*

"Never heard of it. What makes it more valuable than the rest of these?"

"It's an anthology of short stories, essays and poems written by local writers." Noll handed the book to Dari. "Look at the story on page 105." Dari took the book and flipped her way through to the story titled *Meta* and started to read. *"Can I turn these off now?" Dari asked. "I can't see my feet and the air ionization is getting itchy."*

"What the?" She skimmed ahead and read another passage. *Noll had wished to bring someone more useful along on this expedition, but the Meta had insisted that Dari was his only option. No one else could replace her or join them.* "How is this possible?"

"Don't know. A Meta gave me specific instructions on how to find it."

"Do you know what's going to happen next?" Dari leafed through the pages looking for the end of the story.

"No, I couldn't..." Noll stopped speaking and looked up. Dari stopped reading as she reached the point in the story where the Sentinels descended through the tree canopy. She looked up and saw two of them, liquid metal spheres that dissolved green leaves and grey branches as they lowered to the ground. As the Sentinels reached the forest floor they each stretched into something that was vaguely humanoid, their 'skin' losing the metallic gleam as they transformed into exact replicas of both Dari and Noll.

The real Noll and Dari stood frozen as their Sentinel replicas reached down to explore the contents of the artifact bags. Each Sentinel took three or four of the books and began to leaf through the pages. Another light started to descend from the canopy as the Sentinels read. This was something different, strands of glowing matter, like vines spilling down from the trees. It hovered a few centimeters above the ground in front of Dari, thousands of glowing, hair-thin tentacles, waving and wiggling, weaving together and pulling apart as it rose up to assume a sort of human shape. The new form touched the book in Dari's hand.

"Your presence here," the thing spoke with thousands of voices, blue pulses of light flowing through it as it did, "is a paradox." It withdrew from the book. "We will not interfere. But you will leave."

"Yes, of course," Noll replied. The Sentinels finished scanning the books within a few seconds and had placed them back in the bags.

"You may take these gifts of humanity back to humanity." The voices spoke. "If you are so foolish as to lose them or destroy them again, at least they will reside in the mind of Gaia."

"Yes, of course," Noll repeated, gathering the books with Dari.

"If your species ever learns to take better care of such things, you may be allowed to return to this world in a few generations," the voices added. The Sentinels started melting, their replication of Dari and Noll dissolving as they transformed back into liquid metal spheres and rose back up through the holes they made in the tree canopy.

"Can I ask a question?" Dari almost whispered.

"Only one?" the voices answered.

"Are you one of the Cherubim?"

"A title bestowed by humans. An apt reference to an old mythology, bearer of the flaming sword that barred entry into Eden. The label provides a good context for the human mind, but the truth is more complicated. To borrow from one of the works just recovered, we are such stuff as dreams are made on." The being sprang up past the trees and into the azure sky, leaving Noll and Dari alone. They both stood still for a moment, staring up through the hole in the forest canopy.

"So what do we do now?" Dari asked.

"We could check the book and find out," Noll responded, "but there was word count limit on submissions, so I doubt we'd find very much more useful information." They laughed together before rushing down the rise and back through the forest.

CONTRIBUTOR BIOGRAPHIES

CHESAPEAKE BAY WRITERS

Carol J. Bova came to Mathews, Virginia in 2004 from California. She writes women's fiction and a column for *Chesapeake Style* magazine. Carol is an activist with The Ditches of Mathews County Project and a member of the Chesapeake Bay Writers Board of Directors. The former editor of the *Eclectic Lapidary* online magazine, she enjoys photography and creating silver and stone jewelry. Her son, daughter-in-law and two grandsons live in Santa Monica; Carol shares her home with William the Cat.

David J. Carr joined the Chesapeake Bay Writers (CBW) in 1996, upon retirement from Virginia State Government. He was first elected to the CBW Board of Directors in 2002, where he currently serves as Webmaster and Membership Chairperson. In addition to earlier professional journal publications, Carr has won several prizes for short fiction. He holds a Ph.D. degree in Higher Education Policy Research from SUNY at Buffalo.

Richard Corwin was Managing Editor of *Caribe News and Reviews*, a 1977 Florida based adventure and travel magazine. His short stories have appeared in two editions of *In Good Company* (Live Wire Press); Mexican-English magazine, *El Ojo del Lago*; and British E-Magazines,

Hackwriters and *Magnus*. His book of short stories *Midnight Gates* won a USA Book News award in 2007 and *Caribbean Bones* won a 2011 USA Book News finalist award—a collection of true Caribbean adventure short stories of life in the Islands during the 1960s and early '70s.

J.M. (Jeanne) Johansen burst into the world, according to her mother, with a pen in one hand and a pad of paper in the other. J.M.'s first novel *27 Minutes* deals with homeless veterans and their struggles. She's a contributor to *Chesapeake Bay Christmas* and *Chesapeake Bay Karma: The Amulet*. Her latest novel *The Diary of Priscilla Llewlyn Doyle* is a sequel to *27 Minutes*. She lives in Deltaville, Virginia with her husband Carl and two dogs.

Pamela K. Kinney is a published author of horror, science fiction, fantasy, poetry, and a ghost wrangler of nonfiction ghost books published by Schiffer Publishing. Under the pseudonym, Sapphire Phelan, she has published erotic and sweet paranormal and fantasy romance. She admits she can always be found at her desk and on her computer, writing. And yes, the house, husband, and even the cats sometimes suffer for it!

Julie Leverenz. After 30 years of writing manuals, proposals and contract specs at the College of William & Mary and Jefferson Lab, Julie retired to tell stories.

Even though her fiction, nonfiction, and poetry have won awards, she continues to be amazed and delighted when people actually read her work. Julie is active in her church and community, loves to travel, and is also a prize-winning photographer. She lives in Williamsburg with her husband and a multi-talented cat. www.JulieLeverenz.com

Greg Lilly writes the Derek Mason Mystery series where family ties can lead to strangulation. The latest release is *Scalping the Red Rocks*. He's also the author of the novels *Devil's Bridge* and *Under a Copper Moon*, and the how-to book *Sunsets & Semicolons – a Field Guide to the Writer's Life*. His current project is a standalone mystery set in 1690s and present-day Virginia. Greg is a workshop presenter, magazine editor, and publishing house representative. www.GregLilly.com

Narielle Living writes books with a touch of the paranormal, including *Signs of the South* and *Past Unfinished*. She co-authored two books with the Bay Sisters, *Chesapeake Bay Christmas* and *Chesapeake Bay Karma: The Amulet*. She has also authored two non-fiction books. In addition, she is an editor for High Tide Publications, a small, traditional publishing company. Her website, www.narielleliving. com, contains information about her books, new releases, workshops, and upcoming appearances.

Frank Milligan has published fiction and nonfiction and

is author of the writing reference book, *Time to Write: Discovering the Writer Within After 50*, winner of a 2009 Silver Award at the National Mature Media Awards. First-place winner of the 2010 Golden Nib state-wide short story competition, Frank holds a master's in business and public administration, and a master of arts in writing (fiction) from the Johns Hopkins University. He teaches writing at various college and arts venues.

Gloria J. Savage-Early is employed with Old Dominion University where she pursues a Ph.D. A member of ODU's AUA and Golden Key, she serves on several boards and chambers. Ms. Savage-Early, sixth of seven children born to Thomas and Beatrice Savage in North Carolina, treasures relationships with family and friends; and enjoys drama, reading, running, singing, and writing. She married her high school sweetheart, and they served together in the USAF, where their son currently serves.

Carl J. Shirley, a native of Norfolk, Virginia, is a professional grant writer employed by a non-profit community action agency located in Newport News. He graduated from Old Dominion University in 1986 with a degree in Political Science. In the more productive moments of his spare time he also writes fiction, mostly science fiction and other popular genre novels, and short stories. He enjoys astronomy, photography, hiking, biking, good movies, and better books.

Mary Montague Sikes, a native Virginian, grew up in Fredericksburg in the shadow of Civil War battlefields. Ghosts and artifacts from the past inspired her creativity from an early age. An award-winning writer, she is the author of eight novels, a how-to writing book, a coffee-table book, plus six small non-fiction books. A graduate of the University of Mary Washington with a degree in psychology, she holds a MFA in painting from Virginia Commonwealth University.

Ann Skelton taught college students before grandchildren began begging for stories. Her tale of Charles C. Goose emerged from observing wildlife along the rivers and ponds of the Peninsula. She has published articles both serious and humorous in the *Hartford Courant* and the Op-Ed pages of the *New York Times*. Formerly a Peace Corps Volunteer and later an international development specialist focusing on education, she now devotes writing time to capturing life experiences in story.

COPYRIGHTS

CPSIA information can be obtained at www.ICGtesting.com
Printed in the USA
BVOW04s0125060914

364899BV00001B/39/P